Circus Galacticus

DEVA FAGAN

HARCOURT
Houghton Mifflin Harcourt
Boston   New York   2011

Harcourt is an imprint of Houghton Mifflin Harcourt Publishing Company.

www.hmhbooks.com

Text set in 12-point Classical Garamond BT

LIBRARY OF CONGRESS CATALOGING-IN-PUBLICATION DATA
Fagan, Deva.
Circus Galacticus / Deva Fagan.
p. cm.
Summary: Trix's life in boarding school as an orphan charity case has been hard,
but when an alluring young Ringmaster invites her, a gymnast,
to join Circus Galacticus she gains an entire universe of deadly enemies
and potential friends, along with a chance to unravel secrets of her own past.
ISBN 978-0-547-58136-1
[1. Science fiction. 2. Circus—Fiction. 3. Gymnasts—Fiction. 4. Orphans—Fiction.
5. Identity—Fiction.] I. Title.   PZ7.F136Cir 2011
[Fic]—dc22   2011009594

Manufactured in the United States of America
DOC 10 9 8 7 6 5 4 3 2 1
4500319502

For Maureen,
who has always been a stellar friend

CHAPTER 1

Freak

MY PARENTS always told me I was special. The trouble is, I believed them. Just like I believed they'd always be there, and that real monsters didn't exist. Right.

I guess in a way it's true. I'm not like the other girls at Bleeker Academy. But nobody calls me special here. They have plenty of other names for what I am.

"Hey, freak!"

I stop on my way into the gym, turn, and give Della my best guns-cocked-and-loaded stare. Yeah, I've heard the bit about walking away. Trust me; it doesn't work with Della. She's a shark, and I've learned not to bleed.

The hall is crammed with girls, most of them crowding around the large bulletin board. Excited chatter floats across the sea of navy blue jackets and plaid skirts. Della and her cronies have staked out a prime spot right in front of the shiny new poster decorating the board. Two gleaming, golden words sprawl across the top of the page: CIRCUS GALACTICUS.

"Don't look like that, Trix," Della says, sweet and nasty as cough syrup. "We all know you don't really like it here, so we found you a new home, with the rest of the freaks."

I've got a half-formed insult almost ready to fire. It sputters out as I get a good look at the poster. Garishly painted faces leer at me, grotesque and gorgeous. But it's not the alligator man or the green-haired girl who catches my gaze and freezes me there, making me forget even to fight back.

It's the guy in the center, the one in the electric-blue top hat, reaching out as if he could take my hand and pull me right into that glittering page. I swear his smile has more wattage than every billboard in the city. And those eyes . . . It's only a poster, but they remind me, somehow, of the sky out in the desert. Dark and deep and glittering, blazing with possibilities.

Dimly, I'm aware of one of the other girls complaining. "I still don't see why we're going to some stupid circus. This stuff is for kids. They should be sending us to a concert or something."

"At least the ringmaster's hot," someone says, giggling. "Too bad he's stuck in the sequined freak show. He could totally be in the movies."

Bright spots fuzz against my eyelids, and I blink, trying to get back to reality. There's something else at the bottom, under the performance information and promises of popcorn and cotton candy. I lean closer, squinting to read the odd, silvery print.

Feeling alone? Misunderstood? Strange things happening? We have answers! Visit the Hall of Mirrors and find your True Self!

If only. I shake the crazy thought out of my head. It's a line to drum up desperate idiots looking for answers. It's not like some circus mirror can fix my screwed-up life. It can't bring *them* back.

"What's your problem now?" says Della.

"Just reading the fine print," I say, tapping the poster.

Della looks from me to the poster. "There's nothing there, moron."

"Check your eyes, princess. This bit. Right here."

Della turns to her pack and circles her finger beside her ear.

"You seriously can't see this?" I'm too surprised to stay on the defensive.

"God, you really do belong in the freak show," says Della. The rest of the girls crack up.

I'm not sure what Della's playing at, but if I don't start fighting back, this is going to turn into a feeding frenzy. I step away from the poster and shrug. "Thanks for the career counseling, but I've got other plans."

"Other plans?" Della says dangerously. "You mean state finals? As if you have a chance. Especially if you show up looking like some reject from the League of Supergeeks." Her lip curls at my neon-green tights.

Okay, so they have silver lightning bolts running up the side. Sometimes a girl needs to feel like a superhero. It sure beats feeling like the resident crazy girl who has no friends. I cross my arms, matching Della's sharp smile. "At least *I'm* going."

Score. I catch Della's wince before she can shrug it off. "Whatever. *I'm* not some orphan charity case begging for a scholarship," she says. "And I'm not delusional. I hope you still buy your own hype when you're slinging fries."

The other girls giggle. Not only Della's pack, but the rest of the average Janes trying to hold their place in the food chain. If I were a better person, I'd forgive them. Right now I'm just trying not to let Della see how deep that cuts.

"Oh, poor Trix," says Della. "I made her cry."

That's it. If I don't get out of here soon, she's going to be eating that stupid poster and I'm going to be on the fast track to a life of fries. I start off down the hall to class. Okay, so maybe I brush into Della on the way. Just a little.

The next thing I know, I'm flying through the air with the heat of Della's shove burning into my back. I roll, letting my body do what I've trained it to do, even though this is hard linoleum, not padded mats.

I scramble to my feet and throw myself at Della, smashing her into the wall. I pull her back. My fingers twist into the collar of her shirt. Scarlet drops spatter the white cotton. Blood trickles from her nose. I freeze.

It's not a last-minute attack of remorse. It's the look on her face. Triumph. Then a voice speaks.

"Beatrix Ling! What in heaven's name are you doing? Unhand Miss Dimello at once!"

I force my fingers to unclench, even as Della puts on a look of injured innocence.

Headmistress Primwell minces forward, her soft cheeks quivering as she regards the pair of us. Lips compressed, she hands Della a tissue. "Miss Dimello, please explain."

"It was an accident, Headmistress," says Della, slightly muffled as she presses the tissue to her bloody nose. "Trix tripped."

"You pushed me!"

I swear, if Della looked any more innocent she'd have forest creatures frolicking around her feet. "The hallway was crowded," she says. "I tried to help, but she went kind of crazy." Over Della's shoulder I see the ring-master smiling above his invisible promises. My pulse hammers in my ears.

"I'm *not* crazy!"

"Enough, Miss Ling. I think we had best continue this conversation in my office."

* * *

The headmistress's office is a lot like the rest of Bleeker Academy for Girls: shabby, uptight, and depressing. It's November, so it's already dark. The sickly yellow light of a streetlamp trickles in through the dusty window.

I don't sit. Neither does Primwell. The wide oak desk between us holds a writing mat, three pencils sharpened to needle-fine points, and a bowl full of what look like hard candies but are actually nasty menthol throat lozenges.

I wait for her to say something, but she turns her back to me, moving to one of the olive-green filing cabinets lining the back wall. The drawer slides open with a bang that makes me jump. Primwell thumps a hefty file labeled LING, BEATRIX onto the desk, sighing like it's her burden, not mine. "Do you know what this is?"

"My records."

"And do you know, Miss Ling, that your file is approximately five times as thick as that of any other student?"

"I guess I'm just more interesting."

"I should think a girl who owes her room, her board, and her very future to the charity of others would try a bit harder to conform to our standards of behavior." Primwell looks at me like I'm some sort of mangy dog at the pound, the type that's about to get put down because it's too much trouble and no one wants to bother with it any longer. Maybe she *is* sorry for me, but I think she's more sorry for herself.

"Is that too much to ask?" she says. "Can't you try a little harder to make this work?"

"It's not my fault! Della and the rest of them, they act like—"

Primwell cuts me off with a wave of her hand. "Personal responsibility, Miss Ling. That is something we value highly here at Bleeker Academy. Perhaps instead of blaming Miss Dimello and the other girls, you should be asking yourself what you can do to make your life— all our lives—easier."

I set my fists on the desk. "You think this is my fault? You think I can make Della like me? No way. She hates me. It's not my fault I'm going to the finals and she isn't."

"Not anymore," says Primwell.

"What?" She can't mean what I think she means. No. Please no.

"We have had enough of your disruptions. The other students deserve better than this. I'm sorry, Miss Ling, but I'm afraid you will not be attending the state finals. I am removing you from the gymnastics team."

The air in my lungs vanishes, like I've been dumped in a vacuum. "P-please," I finally stammer, "give me another chance. I need to compete. I can get a scholarship, go to college, become an astr—"

She shakes her head. "You dream too large, Miss Ling." She steeples her fingers and looks at me with what she probably thinks is a kindly expression. "Your grades aren't bad. Some are even quite good. But with your history of behavioral issues and"—she coughs—"your financial situation, you have to be realistic about your options. It's not as if you have other prospects."

"I do, too," I insist, reckless with my fear.

Primwell's expression softens for a moment. "Your parents are dead, Beatrix. Clinging to false hopes does you no favors." She flips open my file. I turn away, but not before I see the harsh black headline of the news clipping. TRAGIC ROCKET ACCIDENT CLAIMS LIVES OF ASTRONAUTS.

My heart races. I'm eight again, the little girl in a field in Florida, watching fire and light rage across the sky. I don't quite understand the shrieks and cries from the grownups, except that something is horribly wrong. I'm trapped in that moment when my insides collapsed, a black hole about to suck all the light and joy from my life.

I gulp, hard, forcing the monster inside back into its

cage. I won't let Primwell pity me. I keep it together until I'm back in my dorm room. I force open the dusty, creaky old window with shaking fingers, then collapse against the frame.

Cool air slides over my hot cheeks. I keep my eyes on the lightning bolts decorating my ankles. In my mind, I run through my floor routine. Back handspring, step out, round-off. Twist and flip and whirl. I'm perfect, flawless. The judges applaud. I stand on a step, and someone slings a medal around my neck.

But only in my dreams. I brush a hand across my face. I'm no crybaby, but that scholarship was my last chance, and now it's gone. How can this be my life? Were my folks lying? How could they leave me in this horrible place, thinking I'm something special? Maybe I *am* a deluded freak. I lift my head and stare out the window. The city lights stain the night sky orange. It doesn't stop me from squinting at the fuzzy specks above.

I was six years old the first time I really saw the stars. They hung sharp as broken glass in the desert sky. I jumped, trying to reach them—they looked so *close*. I begged my dad to hoist me up on his shoulders, but even he wasn't tall enough. God, I can still feel that ache. I'd never wanted anything that bad.

Dad smiled and tried to make me laugh away my tears. But Mom understood. She held me so tight I can almost feel her arms, even now, nine years later. I think she was crying, too. *You'll reach them someday, Beatrix,* she said. *I promise.* Then she spun me around until my head swam with stars. That's all I have left of my folks now.

The stars . . . and the rock.

Dad gave it to me that same night. Here's the funny thing: What I remember best about my dad is his smile. He was this big bear of a guy who loved practical jokes and silly puns. But that night he was totally serious.

It's from up there, he said, pointing to the swirl of light above us. *And it's very, very important. There are people who want it. Bad people. You have to keep it secret. You have to protect it. Can you promise to do that, Beatrix?*

So I promised. Crossed my heart, and all that. Mom gave me another hug, then whispered in my ear, *You're our special girl, sweetheart, and only you can keep it safe.*

I wonder sometimes if it was just another of Dad's practical jokes. Maybe it didn't mean anything. Sure, the rock is real enough. And it's not like any meteorite I've seen: smooth and black and glossy, more like something spat out of a volcano. But it's not as if ninjas have been breaking into my dorm room to nab it.

I pull the meteorite out of my sock drawer and set it on the window ledge where it can catch the almost-starlight. I hope they can see I still have it, if they're watching.

"Hey, Mom. Hey, Dad. I don't suppose you guys

could give me some help?" I lean out, trying to catch a glimpse of Orion, my mom's favorite constellation. "I think I screwed up, bad. It's hard, you know, when—"

The words die in my throat as I realize there's a guy across the street watching me. I'm pretty sure it's a guy, even in that long gray coat. He's standing just beyond the ring of yellow light cast by the nearest streetlamp. I can't make out his face. There's a scarf muffling the bottom half, and he's wearing these weird mirrored sunglasses. A thin coil of smoke twists up, catching the light, but I can't see his cigarette.

Okay, maybe he's not watching me. Maybe he's having a smoke. It still creeps me out enough that I shut my window. There are better places to see the stars.

Heat sears my hand as I pick up the rock. I throw it onto the bed. How did it get so blazing hot? I blow on my stinging fingers. I must have put it down too close to the heating pipes.

Wrapping the rock in my blanket, I throw it over my shoulder hobo-style and slip out of my room. If Primwell catches me out, there'll be hell to pay, but it's worth the risk to get closer to the stars. Besides, no one knows about the unlocked door to the roof except me and Eddie, the night janitor. He isn't allowed to smoke on school property but likes to have a quick one at the end of his shift, watching the sun come up over the city. Works for me. I only come up here when it's full dark.

It's not much better than my dorm-room window,

but there's one spot where I can curl up and tilt my head against the chimney and see nothing except the sky. My blanket's thin and ratty, but the rock is still warm, so I press it to my chest and huddle down. I slip into happier memories of spinning under the stars. In this half-dream state I can almost remember what my mom's voice sounds like. *You're our special girl, sweetheart.*

I wake to fuzzy grayness. Thick fog blankets the rooftop, smelling like the sea. It's still the middle of the night. Better get back to my own bed before Primwell catches me and decides to expel me from the school as well as the gymnastics team. I roll upright, bundling the blanket and sticking the meteorite back in my pocket. It's ice-cold now.

Cautiously I find my way to the doorway through the fog, then hustle down the stairs and back to my dorm. I'm two steps through the door when I realize the window is wide open. I spin around as the door thumps closed behind me. A figure steps from the shadows.

I take it back. Ninjas *have* broken into my room.

CHAPTER 2

Nyl

I GRAB for the nearest weapon, an old hockey stick propped by the foot of my bed. I whip it through the air and slam it into the intruder. There's a dull clang. The impact jitters into my arms.

I don't waste time. I'm pulling back for another swing when a word cuts through the dark air.

"Wait." His voice is raspy, like he's talking through an old pipe.

"Yeah, right." I swing. An arm shoots out, seizing the shaft of the hockey stick.

It's him. Creepy smoking guy. I still can't see his face, only the close-clipped black hair, gleaming gray at the temples. His mirrored lenses catch glints of yellow streetlight as he twists, tearing the hockey stick out of my grip. He snaps it in two in midair, then tosses the broken shards across the room. "Don't fight me, Beatrix. I'm not here to hurt you."

I take a step back. My panic-quick pulse beats in my ears. "How do you know my name?"

"I know more than your name. I know you are unhappy. I know who your parents were."

The meteorite suddenly feels heavy in my pocket. "Who *are* you?"

"You can call me Nyl."

"And you're what? Some sort of long-lost family friend? Fairy godfather?"

The choking, wheezing sound nearly jumps me out of my skin before I realize he's laughing. "In a manner of speaking."

"I'm not looking for a prince." Yeah, keep up the banter, I tell myself. Don't let him see how scared you are.

Nyl cocks his head, his voice smoother now. "What about a place where you belong? I can give you that. They left you alone, with so many questions and no answers. I can help you."

I slip a hand into my pocket to grip the meteorite.

The weird silvery words from the poster come back to me. *Strange things happening? We have answers!*

"Are you from the circus?"

"No!" He recoils so violently the scarf slips free from his face. My breath catches at the sight of what's beneath: a chrome faceplate, like some sort of funky gas mask, studded with hoses that curve off over his shoulders. Threads of white smoke rise from behind his back as he draws a rustling breath.

I open my mouth, but it's a long moment before anything comes out. "What—who are you?"

"Someone who knows you can't cover lies with bright lights and sequined costumes." The bitterness in Nyl's voice crawls along my skin. "Don't trust him. That boy may glitter and enchant, but he is far more dangerous than you can imagine. You will find no answers there. Believe me, it will only end in pain."

As I back up another step, I hit the edge of my bed and stumble. The direction of Nyl's gaze shifts to my hand, raised to steady myself. And the meteorite I'm holding.

Smoke twists up from Nyl's silver mask as he growls something I can't make out. His fingers twitch, and I think I see a crackle of blue light in his palm, just for a moment. "That stone. Beatrix, did your parents give that to you? Did they tell you how dangerous it is?"

"My parents wouldn't give me something dangerous," I say fiercely.

"You must give it to me."

Nyl moves so fast I don't have time to run. His cold fingers clamp onto my shoulders, pulling me close. The mirrored lenses of his goggles reflect fragments of my face: a wing of shiny black hair, a dark, terrified eye. His breathing is as loud as a hurricane in my ears.

You have to keep it secret. You have to protect it. Can you promise to do that, Beatrix?

I struggle against his hard, cold grip, wrenching my arm up. The meteorite crunches into his monstrous face. He catches my hand before I can land another blow. Crackling blue flames lick from his fingers, biting into mine. I hiss as pain lances up my arm. The meteorite falls to the floor, skittering off under the bed.

He tries to push me away then, going after the rock. I bring my other arm up. Maybe I can get his eyes, hit a weak spot. My fingers slip across one of the tubes. I grab it and pull. It doesn't give.

Nyl roars, shaking me until my teeth rattle. I bite my tongue and taste blood. Just do it! I scream silently to myself. You promised! You need to keep it safe!

I yank on the tube again. A stream of pale smoke hisses into the air. I twist away as Nyl scrabbles at his face, croaking and gasping.

"You will regret . . . your choice." He sounds like he's about to keel over. He backs away, toward the window. "One day . . . you will beg us . . . for help."

He turns, slipping out the window like a ghost. By

the time I stick my head out to see where he's gone, there's no sign of him. How did he even get up here? My dorm is on the third floor. I slam down the window anyway, busting my fingers to close the ancient lock.

I slump onto my bed. Now that he's gone, now that it's over, I start to shake. Some maniac in a silver gas mask just broke into my dorm room and attacked me with a glowing handful of blue lightning! If there weren't a shattered hockey stick lying in the corner of the room, I'd think I was going crazy. All my life I've been afraid it was all a big joke, my folks saying I'm special and giving me the rock to keep safe. Well, I guess it's not a joke, at least not the part about keeping the rock safe.

The meteorite! I scrabble under my bed until I find it, then slump down to the floor, hugging it to my chest. Breathe, I tell myself. Just breathe.

I curl into bed, trying to push down my host of fears. I can do this. I'll find answers. Things will look better tomorrow; I know it.

When I wake up the next morning, my hair is pink.

* * *

A girl with hair the color of cotton candy stares back from the mirror. I raise a hand to my cheek. So does she. I tug a lock of my hair forward so I can see that, yes, it really is *bright pink*.

At first my mind spins elaborate explanations. Maybe

I got something on me yesterday in chem class that caused a weird reaction. Or Della snuck in and dyed it while I was asleep. Maybe I ate a piece of radioactive bubblegum.

Was this was what Nyl was warning me about? Did the rock somehow cause this? I pull the meteorite from under my pillow. I frown as my fingers catch against a slight imperfection. What the—?

A thin crack runs halfway around the rock. It's barely noticeable, but that doesn't stop the guilt hammering into me. They gave me one thing to do, and I screwed it up. It must have happened when I bashed it into Nyl's face. Or maybe when I dropped it. Doesn't matter—it's still my fault.

All things considered, it's been a pretty miserable twenty-four hours. Getting kicked off the gymnastics team means my ticket out of this sorry excuse for a life is toast. I've got a crazy gas-mask-wearing stalker who can toss around blue lightning with his bare hands. And Primwell is going to flip out when she sees my hair.

Honestly, though, the pink isn't bad. It'd be cute if it weren't so freaktastic having it change color all on its own. What's next, paisley? Or worse, plaid?

That's right, Trix, I tell myself. Hold on to your sense of humor.

I dig out a scarf and tie it kerchief-style over my head. My bobbed hair is short enough that I think that'll do the trick. It's Saturday, so at least there aren't any classes. And since I've been kicked off the team, no practices, either.

I slip downstairs, hoping I don't meet anyone, especially Primwell. But the hall is empty. Just me and my pink hair, and the ringmaster's smile daring me to dream.

I study the poster. What did Nyl say? *Don't trust him. That boy may glitter and enchant, but he is far more dangerous than you can imagine.*

Was he talking about the ringmaster? He looks too young to be dangerous. Too young to be a ringmaster, for that matter. But there's something in his eyes, something ancient and timeless and, yeah, maybe a little scary. Again, I think of the desert sky. Are the stars dangerous?

I wonder what my parents would say.

I shift my gaze down. At the bottom of the page, the silver words still promise answers. And today's date. The school trip is tonight.

"Let's hope for some truth in advertising," I tell the poster. Because you can bet I'm not going just for the popcorn.

* * *

Our buses pull up in front of a giant red striped tent that rises up from a cloud of spinning spotlights. At the top sits a ringed ball, like the planet Saturn, proclaiming

CIRCUS GALACTICUS! with each revolution. I've spent the entire ride scrunched down in my seat, praying Primwell doesn't decide my kerchief is a dress-code violation and discover my pink hair.

I make it off the bus safely, lagging at the rear of the group. An army of smaller stands lines the approach to the big top, decked out in stripes and neon. There's still a ton of people outside, sucking down sodas and cramming popcorn into their mouths. At least I think it's popcorn. It looks blue in this light.

I ditch the school group as they head for the ticket booth. I hustle along the midway, searching for the Hall of Mirrors. Music buzzes against my skin, matching the jittery excitement inside me. I think I see Primwell, so I duck behind a big guy in front of one of the refreshment stands. He doesn't notice; he's too busy shaking his tub of popcorn angrily at the boy inside.

"But it *is* popcorn," the boy is saying. He rubs a hand over his crest of bright red hair. He's got a crazy clown grin slathered over his lips and asymmetrical white diamonds on his cheeks.

The man scowls. "It's blue!"

"Doesn't it taste like popcorn?" says the clown boy, sounding disappointed. "Anyway, that other stuff is blue. The frozen drinks. Slooshies, or whatever you call them. I figured you Earthers liked your food blue."

Earthers? That's carrying this whole space theme a

little far. The boy is trying to soothe Mr. No Blue Popcorn with complimentary "slooshies" when I spot what I'm looking for: a long, low tent slung up alongside the big top. The sign on the front says HALL OF MIRRORS, under a larger neon light that blares FREAK SHOW. I guess the universe has a sense of humor.

I'm about to go for it when I see Primwell. She's patrolling the open thoroughfare between me and my answers with a searching look on her face. And I kind of doubt she's on the prowl for blue slooshies. I bounce on my toes, my stomach a churning ball of frustration.

A loudspeaker crackles. "Ladies and gentlemen, the show is about to begin! Please make your way to your seats, and let us take you out of this world!"

I stop bouncing, mesmerized. It's a voice that makes you want to look up into the starry night sky and spin, or to run a mile to see the first snowflakes falling over the bay. As a tide of bodies surges toward the big top, I lose sight of Primwell. I shake off my daze. It's now or never. I run for it.

Gulping down air, I crouch inside the Freak Show tent, letting my eyes adjust. The only light is the weak golden glow from the glass display cases jammed in everywhere. I move farther in, checking out the labels as I go. It's some crazy stuff. CONSULT THE DRAGON ORACLE. WONDER AT THE LAST BREATH OF PASHFALLASARDOO. There's some disgusting green oil that's labeled OOZE. But no Hall of Mirrors. Probably way at the back. This place is bigger than I thought.

The gold lights near the front of the tent flicker. I duck instantly behind the nearest display, holding my breath. Was that a footstep? I retreat deeper into the tent.

I'm backing up, eyes peeled wide, when my heel crunches onto an empty popcorn tub. The breath catches in my throat as some instinct throws me down. A dark shadow whooshes over me. I come up with my fists clenched to confront my attacker. It's Nyl.

"Oh, wonderful. I needed a few more dire-yet-vague warnings." That's right, Trix, keep up the snappy lines, and maybe you'll forget how terrifyingly weird your life is.

Nyl stares at me. I realize my kerchief is gone, lost in the shuffle. "Your hair . . ." His shoulders droop slightly. "You should have given me the stone when I asked for it, Beatrix. I could have stopped this."

"Don't tell me my pink hair is going to destroy the universe. I mean, it's a little bright, but it's not radioactive."

"If you understood what is at stake, you would not joke."

"Okay, then enlighten me. Are you trying to tell me some space rock turned my hair pink?"

"Yes. And now you need to give it to me before it

corrupts you further. I can still help you, Beatrix. We can cleanse you of the taint. You can be one of us."

"Cleanse me, huh?" I take a step back. He's trying to sound smooth, but I can hear the teeth in his words. This is about to get ugly. "How 'bout I get back to you? I'd like a second opinion, preferably from someone who isn't attacking me."

"There is no more time!"

As he makes a grab for me, I kick the legs of the nearest display. Glass crackles across the ground. A tide of oily green ooze slops out from the smashed display. Nyl sees it, but not in time to avoid it. His foot lands right in the middle of the puddle, and the next moment his legs go flying out from under him.

I run. I don't care about the Hall of Mirrors anymore. I just want out of here. Please, please, let there be an emergency exit.

I can see the rear wall. There's no way out. Only a red-curtained doorway under a big, shimmery sign that says HALL OF MIRRORS. Do I dare go in? What if I get trapped inside? Nyl's breathing rasps so loud I could swear he's right behind me. I risk a look back. Nothing.

In the distance, something clicks, and a whole row of display cases go dark. *Click.* Another row blinks out. *Click.* And another. Pretty soon it'll be pitch-black in here. He's driving me with darkness. I've got nowhere else to run. I push through the curtain.

Warped reflections goggle at me. Turning one way, I see myself impossibly thin with a head like a watermelon. Another, and I'm a potbellied string bean. There's a wiggly Trix, a short Trix, a tall Trix. The only thing they all have in common is hot-pink hair and desperate eyes.

"Okay, I'm here," I whisper to the mirrors. "Where are my answers?" I spin, searching the reflections. "Come on! There was secret writing and everything. It must have meant something. I can't just be going insane."

Nothing happens.

"There's nowhere to run, Beatrix. Stop fighting me."

I bite down hard on the scream that tries to force its way out of my throat. It sounds like he's right on the other side of that red curtain. I back away, until my shoulder blades meet the undulating coolness of the farthest mirror. Nowhere else to run.

The curtain trembles. A gray-gloved hand pushes through. My splayed fingers brush the smooth surface behind me. Then, suddenly, I'm falling backward. Right through the mirror.

CHAPTER 3

Through the Looking Glass

I STUMBLE, trying to figure out what happened. Narrow corridors twist away on either side, cluttered with boxes and bins. An oblong of dark glass fills the wall in front of me.

You dork, I tell myself. It's not a magic portal. It's some kind of secret sliding door. Judging by the jumble of sequined costumes, hoops, and bowling pins, I must be somewhere backstage, inside the big top itself maybe, since I can hear the distant beat of music. Question is, am I safe?

I lean closer to the dark glass, trying to see the room beyond, then leap back. Nyl's right on the other side of the glass, staring at me.

My heartbeat throbs in my ears, the only part of me that isn't frozen, for a long, long moment. Nyl lifts a hand toward the glass. I get the impression he's trying to touch it. Then he clenches his fist, swinging it down to his side.

Can he even see me? I force one arm to move, waving it in front of the mirror. Now that I think about it, this stuff looks a lot like that one-sided glass you see in cop shows.

No reaction. Nyl stands there, staring. Then he turns and stalks out of the room. I don't breathe until the red curtains swing closed behind him. I back away from the mirror door. There's no way I'm going out that way. Besides, the poster promised me answers, and I'm not leaving until I've got some. There's got to be someone here who knows something. The music seems louder to the left, so I head that way.

As I pass the heaps of boxes, I squint at them. The labels are in another language, some crazy alphabet I don't even recognize. But it's that same silvery paint as on the poster. I reach out to touch the letters, only to snatch my hand back. The gibberish is gone, replaced by a perfectly recognizable word: FRAGILE.

Whoa. I try another. HIGHLY DANGEROUS. I back away,

and not only because of the warning. This is freaking me out almost as much as the stalker in the gas mask who wants to "cleanse" me. Maybe it's some kind of optical illusion. I keep going, but I make a point of checking all the boxes as I pass by. Who knows? Maybe one of them will be labeled ANSWERS.

The music is louder, so I must be getting somewhere. I've just found a large barrel to be used IN CASE OF WEEVIX INFESTATION when I hear voices. I can't make them out at first, but as I get closer the words grow clear, like I'm tuning in to the station. I skulk behind a tower of hatboxes labeled PROPERTY OF THE GRAND WAZEER OF DENEB-5, listening.

"I said I would take care of it! Don't worry. No one will find out," says a girl's voice. "I have to go. I'm on next, and they'll miss me if I'm not back soon." A buzz of static crackles, then winks out.

I scope things out over the topmost hatbox. After Nyl, I'm not taking chances. Thankfully, this girl seems relatively normal, or as normal as a person can be wearing a skintight sparkling body suit. She doesn't look very menacing, slumped against the wall with her head in her hands. I think she's crying.

I step out, clearing my throat. "Um. Hi. I'm sorry, but I'm sort of lost back here, and I was wondering—"

The girl whips around, her long black braid lashing the air, trailing red sparks. "Intruder!"

"Hey, I didn't mean to! I'm trying to get out."

"Too late for that, spy. What did you hear? Who are you working for?"

"Nobody!" I back up, closer to the hatboxes. "What, you think I'm some sort of Ringling Brothers secret agent? Look, if you don't want random people showing up backstage, you shouldn't put hidden doors in your Hall of Mirrors."

The girl stares at me. She shakes her head, setting fire to the crimson fiber optics again. "That's impossible. You're an Earther."

There's that word again. "Fine. I guess I'm not finding any answers here. I'll keep looking." I turn back the way I came.

I've gone three steps when something whooshes overhead. The girl lands lightly in front of me, blocking the way. I stare. That was one amazing leap, even for an acrobat.

Sparkles crosses her arms. "No, you're coming with me. You've got questions to answer, Earth Girl."

"I don't know anything! That's why I'm here. You guys said you had answers!"

The girl's eyes narrow. When she jumps this time, I'm ready for her. I scoop one of the hatboxes off the pile and hurl it at the figure flying toward me.

Sparkles tries to twist out of the way, too late. The hatbox explodes on impact with her nose, filling the air with brilliant blue-green feathers. The girl crashes onto the floor. I spin around and hightail it down the corridor.

Each footfall jabs my fury into the ground, propelling me forward. I can't believe I was such a moron! All I've learned about my true self is that I'm angry as a hornet's nest and probably going insane. Nyl was right. That poster was one big lie wrapped up in a pretty package.

I check over my shoulder. Sparkles is chasing me. What's she going to do, turn me over to security? Send me back to Primwell? No way. I put on a burst of speed, skidding around a corner and right smack into someone.

All I see is a pair of eyes that glitter like my memory of the desert sky. Then we collapse in a tangle of elbows and flashy clothing. I struggle to get free. My feet connect solidly with something.

"Have a care—that's fine Denebian silk you're treading on." Even without the loudspeaker, his voice fills the hallway with liquid sound.

I stare. I can't help it. That poster was *nothing* compared to the real thing. Della and her girls got one thing right: He could totally be a movie star. He'd melt a million hearts with that smile. It's not only good looks; it's something more, a spark so raw and powerful it shakes my core. I feel like my universe suddenly got a whole new dimension.

"And who do we have here?" he asks, quirking a brow at me. Pounding feet announce Sparkles.

"Ringmaster!"

He looks away from me, finally, and I try to shake off the feeling that I've been standing there for hours rather than seconds. "Yes, Sirra? Is there a problem?"

"This Earth girl was snooping around the back corridor!"

"Snooping isn't necessarily a bad thing. I encourage a good snooping now and again. Keeps us on our toes." He doffs his electric-blue top hat, bowing low. "Welcome to the Big Top. I'm the Ringmaster. And you are . . . ?"

"Beatrix Ling," I manage to get out.

"She's a spy," insists Sparkles—or Sirra, if that's her name. Her nose is red and starting to swell, and she's got blue-green feathers stuck in her hair. She looks like an angry parrot. "And she's a liar. She said she came through the mirror."

"Did she? That *is* interesting."

"It's impossible. She's not one of us!"

"The Tinkers' Mirror never lies. And it's time we had a new recruit to liven things up around here."

"No," protests Sirra. "You're going to bring her *with* us? We're in enough trouble already without taking home souvenirs."

"Hey!" I interrupt. "Nobody's bringing me anywhere! First you make me think I'm crazy with your secret messages, and now you're going to kidnap me? *We have answers,* hah! For all I know, you're the ones who gave me this bubblegum dye job, not my—" I stop myself before I mention the meteorite in my pocket. I've got enough trouble without these bozos coming after it, too.

The Ringmaster cocks his head. "You mean to say your hair isn't normally pink?"

"Of course not! No one has pink hair *naturally!*"

"I grant you it is rare, yes. The Mandate were so dreary in their color choices." He tugs out a lock of his own dark brown hair and studies it mournfully.

My anger is starting to wear off, which isn't a good thing, because that'll leave me with just the fear. My legs tremble. "Please, let me go. I won't cause any trouble."

"I find that hard to believe," says the Ringmaster, casting aside his lighthearted humor with such absolute suddenness it catches the breath in my chest. "You've been causing trouble all your life, haven't you? Asking questions that weren't in the textbooks. Saying things other people were afraid to say. There was always something off about you, something different, something that made other people stare and whisper and maybe even laugh . . . Isn't that right?" His eyes pull on mine, demanding an answer.

I swallow against the boulder that seems to have lodged in my throat. "How . . . how do you know?"

"I know because it's the story of every person who walks through that mirror. It's the story of the Tinker-touched. That's what we are. That's what you are. It's why your hair is that remarkable and quite fetching color, and why you were able to find your way into the Big Top."

I shake my head. "I don't know what you're talking about. I'm . . . nobody. A weirdo. A freak."

"Just like the rest of us."

Sirra snorts. The Ringmaster ignores her, his eyes fixed on mine. Then he grins, twirling his jeweled baton from hand to hand. "But I've gone about this all wrong. You should see the show first. Speaking of which—you'd better get back to the stage, Sirra, before Nola has a fit looping that intro."

I realize that the music has started to repeat, going from a trembling hush to a triumphant burst of synthe-sized trumpeting over and over again, with a grating fuzz of static in between. Sirra hurries away down the corridor, shooting me a backward glance that says pretty clearly she'd rather be bashing my face in.

"Well? Do you want to see the show?" The Ring-master waves for me to follow.

I cross my arms. "Who are you guys, really? You said you had answers. I want answers before I go anywhere."

"We're exactly what it says out front. The Circus Galacticus, bringing acts to delight and amaze across the universe."

"Across the *universe*. Seriously?"

"Of course not!" He gives a huff of disdain. "Do I look like the serious sort? Across the universe stupendously. Across the universe *insouciantly*. Wonderful word, *insouciant*, isn't it? I love Earth. All the brilliant, maddening words. Did you know there are more than six thousand languages on this planet? Drives the translator to distraction."

"Wait; back up. So you're saying you're aliens? I don't . . . I can't . . ."

"Of course you can," says the Ringmaster. "Is it so hard to believe there might be something more out there?"

"No. I mean, my parents always said there was. But . . ." I flap my hands, unable to express just how different this all is from the sleek rocket ships and wise visitors from the stars that figured in my bedtime stories. "A *circus?*"

"You would have preferred an invasion fleet? Flying saucers and death rays?" He gives me a cheeky grin. "Come to the show. You won't regret it."

I feel like I'm standing on the edge of a very deep chasm, and I'm not sure yet if I'm wearing a parachute. I stuff one hand into my pocket, feeling for the reassuring heft of the meteorite. "All right. I'll watch the show."

"Brilliant!" The Ringmaster seizes my hand. The next moment we're careening along the hallway in a madcap dash. I feel giddy, like I've got soda fizzing through my veins. We come to a halt in front of a wide doorway. It opens to reveal a vast darkness sprinkled with blazing lights.

"Welcome to the Big Top," says the Ringmaster, leading me out. We're in a kind of alleyway between two banks of bleachers. Craning my neck, I catch glimpses of sneakers and jeans above. Drifts of blue popcorn and discarded candy wrappers litter the sheet-metal floor on either side. Ahead, a ring of red and blue lights marks the open center of the tent. It's empty. The Ringmaster points his baton upward. "There."

Two silver figures spin through the air, swooping and falling. Spotlights arc across the darkness, tracking the aerial dance. Sirra flips off her trapeze, spinning through the air, once, twice, and she's still going. I count each somersault, amazed. What, does gravity not apply to this girl?

I exhale as she catches hold of her partner's arms, and the crowd erupts with cheers. "Seven midair somersaults? That's impossible. She's . . . she's not flying, is she?"

"Not exactly. Sirra does have a special relationship with gravity, though. It's a remarkable gift, but not everyone in the universe would see it that way. That's why she's here. That's why we're all here, in the Circus Galacticus. Have you ever heard what the best place is to hide something?"

"In plain sight?"

He grins. "Precisely. Out on the street a man with scaly green skin is a monster, a danger, something to be locked up and studied. But stick him under a tent and call him the Spectacular Dragon Boy, and everyone is perfectly willing to believe it's only special effects and makeup. That it isn't real."

I tear my gaze from the aerial display. "Okay, let's say I believe you're aliens and all that. Aren't there planets full of dragon people?"

"Not many," says the Ringmaster. "Not since the Mandate."

"The who?"

"An ancient and terrible power. They held the entire universe in their grasp, once upon a time. They shaped it for eons, molding conformity, establishing law, dictating order on even the most basic genetic levels. It's thanks to them that you and Sirra look like you could be schoolmates, even though you were born in different galaxies."

"Except I've got pink hair now."

He nods. "The Mandate were not the only power at work. There were others who saw diversity as a strength, not a weakness. Where the Mandate created order and conformity, the Tinkers spread color, vitality, and variation. The seeds of their genetic manipulation have been passed down through generations. And when those seeds bloom, you get someone like Sirra. Or someone like you, Beatrix."

"You think my pink hair is some kind of mutation? Are you sure it's not because of something else?" Like, say, a mysterious black meteorite?

He hesitates, but only for a moment. "The Tinkers' Mirror is keyed to specific genetic patterns. There's no way you could have come through it if you weren't touched by the Tinkers."

"But my hair only changed color last night!"

"Right on time, then. Most of the troupe had their gifts flare up in their teens."

Okay, so maybe I'm not a big fake with a space-rock makeover. Maybe I really do belong here. The sharpness of how badly I want that scares me enough that I figure I better change the topic. "So, I'm guessing the Mandate and the Tinkers weren't best friends."

"No. Not at all." The Ringmaster looks down, buffing the brass buttons of his blue tailcoat. "There was a war. A terrible war. And when it was over, they were both gone. All that remained were their children, those carrying the genetic inheritance of the ancients. And the younger races, who banded together, set themselves up a government, and confiscated anything touched by the Tinkers or the Mandate. If they knew what we were, they might lock us away. Or worse, use us, control us, make us their tools."

"So you're outlaws. Mutant outlaws. And now I'm one, too?"

"Exciting, isn't it? Admittedly, it's unlikely the Core Governance will be waltzing in to arrest you anytime soon. Earth is in the Excluded Territories, outside their domain. You could go on with your life, dye your hair so no one notices. Live so no one notices."

"Or . . . ?" I desperately want there to be an "or."

"Or you could come with us. Travel the stars! Spread wonder and amazement across the universe!"

Something deep inside me unfolds, like a crinkly butterfly testing its wings. I still have questions, though. "Hold on. If you really are an intergalactic circus, where's your spaceship?"

"Here." The Ringmaster spins to take in the bleachers, the ring, the tent. "The Big Top can be a slow old girl, but she's reliable and spry when she needs to be." He pats the wall. "She's our home. And she could be yours, too."

A wild burst of applause drowns out anything I might say to that. Sirra and her partner slither down from the heights on ropes of light.

"Time for the grand finale," says the Ringmaster. "Think about it, Beatrix. The choice is yours."

He bounds off toward the ring. The spotlights leap onto him, catching in the large gem at the top of his baton. He twirls it from right hand to left and back again.

I can feel that entire tent watching him. Hundreds, maybe thousands of people. He's like an eclipse: You don't want to look away, even if it dazzles you forever.

"Ladies and gentlemen!" His voice booms out to fill the tent. He turns to take in all the crowd, blue coattails flaring. "It has been our honor to entertain you. If you have learned one thing this night, let it be that anyone can reach the stars. Choose your own destiny, and the universe is yours."

He stops, the tip of his baton pointing directly at me. He gives the slightest nod. "But for now, good night, and may your skies be always bright with stars."

The pulsing music reaches into my chest and grabs my heart, sweeping it away. Figures spill into the ring, colorful and chaotic as a kid's finger painting, cartwheeling and backflipping and dancing. Girls toss rings, leaping through them. Everywhere I turn there's motion and light and life.

Trying to take it all in is like watching a dozen TV screens at once. My feet are stuck fast to the ground, but my heart swoops up into the sky. I could be one of them. If I dare. What have I got to lose?

I spot the redheaded clown who was selling the popcorn. He springs up into the air to land at the top of a pyramid of performers. A gasp reverberates through the stands as every one of their costumes turns silver. It's a rocket. They're forming a human—alien—spaceship. Sparks blossom along the base. A lump clogs my throat.

I close my eyes. I can't watch. My mind is in that Florida field, my eyes seeing that fire again and again and—I can't breathe. I want to run. Lights flare so bright I can see them through my eyelids.

The thunder of applause fills the tent. Then some jolly please-leave-in-an-orderly-fashion music comes on. I open my eyes in time to see the Ringmaster returning from the now-dark ring. I turn away quickly, before he can see my brimming tears.

"Beatrix?"

He actually sounds worried. I allow myself one shuddering, breathless sob. My parents might not have reached the stars, but I can. And I will. I brush my cheeks, put on my smile, and turn back around.

"I'm coming with you. I'm running away to join the circus."

CHAPTER 4

Up, Up, and Away

THE DOORS SKIM SHUT, cutting off the boppy music and the chatter of the departing crowds. "So what happens next?" I ask. "Don't tell me I need to wear one of those skintight glitter suits."

The Ringmaster laughs, twirling his baton. "A tour first, I think. You'll want to get to know your new home and meet the rest of the troupe."

Running footsteps approach along the corridor. There's a girl pelting toward us. She doesn't look any more like an alien than the rest of them. Wavy brown hair, medium brown skin. No tentacles.

"Am I late? Is this her? Did you hear Sirra's intro, Ringmaster?" The girl makes a disgusted face. "I tried to loop it, but the join was all scratchy. It'll be better next time. I know exactly how to fix it . . ." She spews a breathless stream of what sounds like alien gibberish except for a few recognizable words like *wavelength* and *harmonic*.

The Ringmaster lets her babble on, nodding and smiling in a way that makes me think he doesn't understand her any better than I do.

"So that sounds like it ought to work, doesn't it?" she finishes brightly.

"We are fortunate to have your technical genius on board, Nola. I shudder to think what we would do without you."

"Me, too," says Nola cheekily. "We all know you're hopeless without the autosalon. I saw your hair last time the system went haywire. Do you even know how to use a comb?"

The Ringmaster stifles a choking sound. "Right, then. Nola, this is Beatrix, the newest member of the Circus Galacticus."

The girl beams. "Hi! Nola Ogala. I'm a Tech." She points out a gold patch on the shoulder of her black jacket, which looks like a wrench giving off a shower of sparks. "So are *you* the one who bopped Sirra on the nose?"

"Um, yeah." My stomach drops. Don't tell me everyone here is on Team Sirra and I'm just trading one personality cult for another.

She grins. "Hah! I wish I could have seen it. So, do you have a roommate yet? Because I've got a double right now, and it's only me."

Okay, this is *so* much better than Bleeker already. This is where I belong. I can't believe I even listened to that garbage Nyl was trying to—

Nyl. Who couldn't get through the secret superhero door. Who is probably one of the bad guys. Who is *right outside this ship.*

"The Mandate," I say. "I think they're here."

Nola's eyes go big as spotlights, matching her open mouth.

"The Mandate?" repeats the Ringmaster in a tight voice. "Are you sure?"

"Well, it wasn't like he was wearing the T-shirt, but based on the things he said, yeah."

"What sort of things?" asks the Ringmaster.

"For starters, he really doesn't like you. He said you were dangerous."

A hint of a smile pulls at the Ringmaster's mouth. "Hmm. Well, I won't argue with that. Anything else?"

"He"—I almost mention the rock, but chicken out—"he said that my pink hair was a taint he needed to cleanse. Not that he's the picture of normal with that gas mask thing. Plus, he was pretty much the walking definition of creepy. He showed up in my dorm room in the middle of the night! And then he turned up here again, right before the show. My own personal crazy masked stalker."

All the humor washes out of the Ringmaster's face. "Masked? Did he tell you his name?"

"Nyl. Does that mean something to you?"

"It means the Mandate *are* here. And it's time we were leaving." The Ringmaster taps his baton. The jewel on top springs open. There's a panel underneath that looks kind of like a TV remote. As he punches buttons, the lights along the ceiling turn orange and a siren begins wailing somewhere. When he speaks, his voice echoes on all sides.

"Galacticus Crew, this is the Ringmaster speaking. I'm afraid we've run into a small wrinkle. Please prepare for immediate departure and possible evasive maneuvering." He takes off down the corridor.

"Come on," says Nola. "We'd better go, too. He'll need help."

The Ringmaster doesn't slow down, not even when we round a bend and hit what looks like a dead end. The doors peel back, revealing a large space full of light. The Ringmaster darts inside, waving his baton as if directing an invisible orchestra. Lighted panels wink and blink in nonsensical patterns.

"Where are we?" I ask.

"The bridge." Nola pulls me to one side. "Better buckle up. Quick getaways aren't usually the smoothest."

She runs a hand across the wall. An instant later, the surface folds open, revealing two seats. Nola prods me into one of them.

The moment I sit, a belt snakes out across my waist, followed by two more crisscrossing my chest. "Hey!"

"Stay there, where it's safe!" Nola races off to one of the panels and begins tapping at it. "I've got the drives coming up, Ringmaster. We'll be ready in ten."

The Ringmaster is talking into his baton again, sounding as relaxed and cheerful as ever, all while jumping around like a madman at the consoles. "Ladies and gentlemen, in thanks for your splendid patronage, the Circus Galacticus is pleased to offer you free refreshments outside! So hurry up and exit the main tent to claim your popcorn, cotton candy, and slushies. Thank you, and we hope you enjoyed the show!"

"That did it," Nola says after a minute. "Everyone's out. Closing the main doors now."

I tug against the straps holding me in the chair. *Safe* is apparently the alien word for *stuck*. And I can't shake the feeling that somehow this is all my fault. "Can't I do anything? I feel stupid just sitting here."

"First day and she's already raring to go," says the Ringmaster. "I like it." He waves the baton in my direction. "Mind your head." A screen drops down, barely missing my nose. "There. If you could locate our Mandate visitor, I would be most obliged."

It looks a lot like a video game console, complete with joystick, but the screen is dark and the buttons are covered in more alien script. Gingerly, I tap the edge of the display. The gibberish blurs, then reforms. One button now reads POWER. I push it, and the screen crackles to life. I'm looking out at the street, at a line of buses.

Tweaking the joystick shifts the image. Now I'm goggling down at the people in front of the Big Top as they crowd around the refreshment booth. The red-headed clown is handing out striped bags of popcorn and billowing cones of cotton candy.

"Jom, time to fly," says the Ringmaster. On my screen, the boy nods, tossing the last few bags at a pack of little kids, who cheer. He sprints off the screen into the Big Top.

I spin the joystick and curse myself for not saying something sooner. This is my fault. The Ringmaster handed me a ticket to the universe, and I returned the favor by leading his biggest enemy right to him. Nyl could have called up a whole army of other nasties by now. I clench the joystick tightly. No. I *refuse* to lose all this, not after I've just found it.

I'm passing over the chain-link fence along the rear of the circus grounds when I catch a flash that doesn't belong. A sleek black shape sits nearly hidden between a couple of trash bins. "Whoa. Now *that's* a spaceship."

The Ringmaster looks up, frowning. A tap on his

baton, and suddenly one whole wall vanishes, replaced by the image on my screen. "The Mandate have such mundane concepts of spacecraft design."

"It's only one guy." I breathe a sigh of relief. Jiggling the joystick, I zoom in on the dark figure standing near the arrow-sharp nose of the craft. Nyl.

"One is enough."

"You're a million times bigger than he is. And you've all got superpowers. Can't we just . . . fight him? Or something?"

I'd swear the Ringmaster looks afraid for a moment. "We've done what we came here to do. Time to be off. The universe awaits!" He gives the baton a last twirl, ending with a triumphant jab at the console.

The walls shudder. The overhead lights blink from orange to purple. Nola throws herself at the seat beside me. The small screen slides up into the ceiling. On the wall, Nyl's rocket starts giving off sparks from its tail end.

"He's going to follow," calls Nola.

"Let him try." The Ringmaster holds his ground, even as the entire room shifts. "Off we go!"

A huge weight presses down, stealing away my breath. I grip the arms of my seat.

"It's okay," Nola says through chattering teeth. "All perfectly normal."

Suddenly the weight is gone. My insides lurch as gravity shifts. The room spins. Please, please, don't let me get sick.

Then I forget about my stomach entirely as a field of stars opens up across the wallscreen. In one corner looms a gray, pockmarked surface, more detailed than I've ever seen, even through Dad's telescope.

"The moon!"

"Yes, one does tend to run into such things in space," says the Ringmaster. His smile drops away. The gleam in his eyes catches me like the flare of a comet across the sky. "What do you think, Beatrix? Are you glad you came along?"

My heart is too full. I feel like a tongue-tied little kid. I'm such a dork. I can't even speak—all I can do is stare, at him, at the stars.

And then at the sleek black arrow racing onto the screen. "He's back!"

"Drives full up, Ringmaster," calls Nola.

I lean forward as blue light flares along the nose of the Mandate ship. "He's shooting at us!"

"Too late," says the Ringmaster. "Say goodbye to the Earth, Beatrix."

I get one glimpse of a blue and white marble hanging against the blackness of space. Then everything melts: the stars and the bridge and the ship about to shoot . . .

* * *

I blink crud from my eyes. I'm still in the chair on the bridge, but the straps are gone.

"Do you feel okay?" Nola's voice buzzes in my ear.

"Sure. If 'okay' covers feeling like you've been dunked in glue and held upside down for a few days." I groan.

"Jump sickness is always worst the first time. You'll get your space legs quick enough."

"So I guess we got away. Where's the Ringmaster?"

"Oh, you know. Well, actually you *don't*, being new. The Ringmaster never stays in one place very long. He knows the Big Top better than any of us. Always off doing something." She shrugs. "He asked me to take you on a tour. If you feel up to it, that is."

"I am the uppest of the up. If I spend another minute in this chair, I'll grow a drink holder."

"Good! What do you want to see first? There's the common room or the biohabitat or the infirmary or—"

"Can we see outside? Can we see real space?"

"The viewing deck it is!"

A few minutes later, I'm gripping the viewing deck railing and taking deep breaths. I am *not* starting my new life on the Big Top as the girl who faints at the first sight of space. But it's so huge, and I'm so small. Yet at the same time, here I am. In a spaceship! In the middle of it all! Wherever that is.

"What system is this?" I ask. "I don't recognize anything."

Nola taps into a small console along the railing. Lines of blue alien gibberish fly up across the transparent bubble of the viewing deck, labeling each of the stars. "Oops!" She taps a few more buttons. "There, can you read that?"

"Um. Yeah." Most of the stars don't even have labels, and those that I can see are nothing but strings of numbers and letters. "We must be pretty far from Earth if they ran out of names. Are we even still in the Milky Way?"

"Oh, no. That's all part of the Excluded Territories. We're back in Core space now, all quarter-million inhabited systems of it. But here, we can zoom out." She fiddles with the console. The blue lines dance around, reforming a sort of inset star chart. Squinting, I see a tiny blob in the corner labeled *Milky Way*. The larger area is now labeled *ACO 3627*. Good thing I did my last science project on the Great Attractor. At least I recognize something out here.

"We're in the Norma galaxy cluster? We just traveled 250 million light-years? This is one fast ship. Like, impossibly fast. How do you beat light speed?"

"It's more like bending space than going really fast. And we're not sure exactly how it works," admits Nola. "The Tinkers and the Mandate knew how, and this is a Tinker ship. The only one left, as far as we know. Most everything was destroyed in the War. There are a couple of Mandate ships kicking around, too, we think."

"You think? I thought they were, y'know, your big ancient enemy."

"Yeah, but they keep a pretty low profile. They don't

want to get nabbed by the Core Governance any more than we do."

I tap my fingers against the railing. "So what are they doing?"

Nola shrugs. "Gathering strength. Trying to stay in one piece. Same thing as we are, but without the sequins and popcorn. The Core may not like either of us, but it doesn't stop the officials from appropriating any Tinker or Mandate tech they can grab. They'd love to get their hands on the Big Top, if they could find a way around the Ringmaster's lawyer."

"So if there are only a few of these space-bending ships, what does everyone else do? Hitchhike?"

"They use the pipelines. The Mandate set them up eons ago, using some sort of wormhole technology. Regular ships pop in one end and out the other. Most systems have at least one, except where the fighting was really bad during the War." Nola frowns. "You look confused. Is the translator going wonky? Sometimes it takes a while to come back to speed after a jump."

"No, I got it. It's just . . . mind-blowing. I mean, interstellar plumbing!" I wave at the star field. "Which one's yours?"

"Oh." Nola coughs. "It's that one." She zooms in on one of the oblong galaxies in the midsection of the cluster, then points to a star along the edge. "Yamri. Pretty humdrum. The only thing we're famous for is agricultural machinery."

"How long since you left?"

"Five hundred and twenty-three days." She sighs. "I don't even remember what it smells like in the spring. That's when all the fields start blooming up, all green and gold. It was my favorite time of year."

She has a look on her face like Dad used to get whenever I begged him to tell me stories about growing up in Taiwan. He'd tell me about lanterns that asked riddles and filled the night with color, about hiking through misty green mountains, and the sweet crispness of sugarcane juice on a hot day. It was like this magical fairyland that he'd never get back to, not really. "Sorry," I say. "I guess you miss it?"

She shrugs it off. "Oh, it's not that bad. I love the Big Top. I've seen things a colony girl from Yamri would never even imagine. This is where I mean something. This is where I belong." She taps her sparky wrench badge proudly. "Speaking of which, we ought to get you some things. Come on."

CHAPTER 5

The Arena

NOLA LEADS ME THROUGH a maze of wheezy lifts, twisty corridors, and slithery ladders. I don't know how she keeps track of where we are. At one point I'm sure we're about to head back onto the bridge, but instead we end up in an oval room lined with giant iridescent kites.

"Spacewings," says Nola, pausing. She tucks back her wavy crop of brown hair. For the first time I notice the black gadgetry thing looped over her right ear. She fiddles with it. A slip of something dark and flexible slides out to cover her eye, like an odd black eye patch. As I watch, Nola waves her hands in the air, says "Dispensary," then waves some more. She nods and the eyepatch snaps back.

"Okay, we should be able to go this way." She pushes aside a pile of the spacewings, revealing a doorway. "Sorry for the roundabout route, but we're still decompacting after the performance and the jump. Lots of rooms are still smashed flat."

"Decompacting?"

"To make room for the inside of the tent and the jump burst."

"You mean every time you perform, you have to squash down half the ship?"

Nola nods. "And even more when we need to jump. I helped fix some of the compactors after I came on board. We're up to sixty-eight percent now," she says proudly, leading me down yet another tunnel-like corridor. "If only the Ringmaster weren't such a pack rat, we could do much better." She wrinkles her nose. "Plus, there are parts of the ship even the Ringmaster can't get into. Who knows what's in there, gumming up the works? Poor Big Top." She pats the nearest wall.

The wall hums back.

I stop walking. "What was that?"

"Oh, you know, the Big Top likes being appreciated."

"Are you telling me it's *alive?*" I flinch away from the walls slightly.

"Honestly, we don't really know what the Big Top is. I mean, she's older than some planets. But the Tinkers made her and she's partly organic, so . . . yeah, she's alive. Okay, here we are." Nola leads the way through an arched doorway that suddenly looks a lot more like an esophagus than it did a moment ago.

I can't actually see the walls. It looks like someone crammed the contents of about twenty thrift stores into a single room. I step gingerly around a set of giant-size Tinkertoys, a stack of holographic photographs, and a pile of orange bowling pins.

"Sorry about the mess." Nola pushes aside a rocking chair that's got tiny wings sprouting from its back. It rolls back and forth, knocking into a box covered in pipes, which starts tooting off-key and letting out puffs of purple steam.

"What *is* all this stuff?"

"This is people—and by people I mean the Ringmaster—getting carried away with the dispenser." Nola plucks an umbrella off a freestanding console near the center of the room and glares at it. "Oh, I need a new acid-proof umbrella," she goes on in a fake drawl. "No, that's not the thing. What about something in mauve? No, that won't do. Let's try lime green this time, to match my costume." Nola tosses the umbrella aside. "I keep telling people we shouldn't use it willy-nilly until we figure out how to put things back if we don't want them. When we all die smothered by acid-proof umbrellas, then they'll wish they'd listened."

She looks so fierce I hold up my hands. "Um, maybe we shouldn't bother, then. I don't need an acid-proof umbrella. Do I?"

"No." Nola smiles. "But you'll definitely need a know-it-all." She taps the black thing curled around her ear. "Your insignia will have to wait."

"Insignia? You mean that?" I point to the patch on her jacket.

"Right, I'm a Tech. The wrench is our symbol. One sec." She scrambles over to a monstrous pile of clothing and begins rooting through it. A few moments later she's back with her arms full of fabric. "There are four different insignias. See, this one's for the Clowns." Nola holds up a purple jacket with a patch on the shoulder that looks kind of like a Mardi Gras mask. "And this one's for the Principals." She points to the star decorating the end of a long scarf. "And then there's the Freaks," she finishes, holding up a poncho with a decoration that makes me shudder.

"I am *not* wearing an eyeball."

"You won't be wearing anything until we figure out where you belong."

"Didn't the mirror-door whatsit do that already?"

"Coming through the door means you're Tinker-touched. It doesn't tell us anything about how you'll fit into the show. Like if you'll be technical crew, or a supporting performer, or whatever. Can you do anything really neat? Bend gravity or turn water to ice? Oooh, can you control electricity? That would be amazing!"

I swallow a sudden lumpy feeling in my throat. What if I can't do anything? What if I'm not the real deal, just some wannabe spiffed up by my meteorite somehow? Are they going to drop me off with a "Sorry, go back to school, get a job selling pizza, have a swell life?" Or worse, will I end up stuck in a glass box under a sign: MARVEL AT THE PINK-HAIRED GIRL?

I shrug, hoping it looks casual. "My hair turned pink. That's it so far. Anyway, what do you do? I mean, how did you figure out you were a Tech?"

"I've always been good with machines and that stuff. My aunt swears I fixed her combine when I was only five. By the time I was twelve, they were hiding me whenever Core inspectors came around. Didn't want them to see me doing this." Nola holds out her hand.

I gasp. Tiny silver ridges appear across her palm. In a moment her whole hand looks like something from the inside of a computer. Nola wiggles her fingers, laughing. "Weird, huh? I thought everybody could do it at first. I did all sorts of neat stuff. I programmed our auto-cook to put extra syrup in my porridge; I set the video-com to switch over to *Love Among the Stars* whenever a new episode came online. It was great!"

Nola heads for the birdbath-shaped console poking up from the center of the room. "We'll have to request your know-it-all from the dispenser," she explains, laying her still-silvery palm on the console. "Now you put your hand there, so it can read your genetic signature."

I set my hand alongside Nola's. With a snick of sliding metal, the hollow opens, popping out a small pile of black gadgetry.

"Go on," says Nola. "Try it out."

Gingerly, I hook the loop over my ear.

"WELL, HELLOOO, PARTNER!"

"Aaagh!" I try to pull it off, but the band clamps into place along my forehead.

The synthetic voice babbles on. "I know we're going to be the best of friends, dear! I can't wait to tell you *everything* about the universe! Are you excited? I know I am! Now, what should we cover first, hmmm? Ooooh, you must be *dying* to know the latest dish from *Love Among the Stars;* am I right? In the last episode, we saw Dalana admit her true feelings to Kel Starstrike, just before the space pirate Zendalos tossed them both into a black hole."

"Shut up!"

"I know! *What* a plot twist! But it gets better,

because meanwhile, Dalana's evil twin, Talana, was scheming to take over the galactic empire by—"

"No, really," I say. "Shut. Up." I yank at the earpiece, but it won't budge.

Nola's doubled over, giggling.

"A little help, please?"

"Wow. I knew the know-it-alls have personality chips, but I've never seen one like that."

"It's not funny! How do I get the stupid thing off? I need a new one."

Nola wipes her streaming eyes, no longer laughing. "Oh, Trix, I'm sorry, but I can't. We only have so many blanks, and once the dispenser imprints it to your genetic code, it can't be reused except by someone from your planet. We can't just make a new one."

"Well, then, can you at least give this one a new personality chip?"

"Not easily. But I'm sure this one will settle in, given a few days."

"Given a few tranquilizers, maybe."

"You can turn it off, if you want to." Nola indicates a button on her own.

"Wait!" protests my know-it-all. "We need to talk about what you're going to wear tomorrow. It's your first full day on ship! We have to look our best, don't we?"

"No, we don't!" I flick the switch. Blessed silence follows. "Hallelujah."

Nola swallows a last giggle. "Seriously, though, Trix. You need a know-it-all."

"Yeah. Because it's vitally important that I know the latest plot twists on *Love Among the Stars*?"

"It's a good show," Nola says with an injured expression. "You ought to try watching. Anyway, it's more than that. Your know-it-all will help you find your way around the Big Top, and you can use it to send messages, like if you need me. Have your know-it-all patch you through to mine. They've got access to the whole datanet."

"I think I'll fly solo for a little longer. So what now?" I yawn. "What time is it, anyway?"

"Your know-it-all could tell you," Nola says with a cheeky grin. "It's ten. Breakfast is at eight."

"So do you sleep in normal beds or what? Don't tell me it's some kind of weird pod thing."

"No, the dorms are really nice. And I meant what I said before. I've got a double. You can room with me if you like."

"Seriously? You mean it?"

"Sure. What, do you snore or something?"

"No, it's just . . ." No one's ever gone out of their way to be friendly to me. I mean, there were some girls at Bleeker who were nice enough—but only when Della wasn't looking. Part of me doesn't think Nola could really want to hang out with me. Crazy, huh? I'm on a spaceship, in another galaxy, and the thing that's hardest to believe is that I've got a shot at my first real friend.

"I'd love to be roommates," I say finally.

Nola beams. "Wait until you see our room. It's the best! I've put in a ton of customizations. You'll love it! I mean, I hope you will."

"I bet it's amazing. So, is that our next stop?"

She shakes her head. "There's no way to reach the dorms right now. We have to wait for the decompaction bell. Everybody's probably hanging out in the commons. Come on, I'll introduce you."

Nola's know-it-all leads us back out past the space-wings, then up two sets of ladders and down a pearly white corridor that spirals like a giant snail shell. We come out into a large round room with mirrored walls, like an inside-out disco ball. About thirty other kids are gathered around a raised platform lit by orange lights. Inside, a figure jumps and catapults as puffs of smoke, bursts of flame, and several nasty-looking metal mallets chomp through the air. I guess "hanging out" in an intergalactic circus involves more than flopping onto the sofa and watching bad TV.

"Someone's in the Arena!" says Nola, clapping her hands together. "Oh. It's Sirra. Well, it's still fun to watch." She leads the way to a spot along the side with a good view. With Sirra putting on a show, nobody pays us much attention.

The Galacticus crew all look about my age or a few years older and oddly normal, for aliens. You could have pulled most of them off the street back home, if you were in the artsy, punked-out part of town. And then there are the really weird ones.

I try not to stare at the guy who looks like a walking boulder, or the one with antennae like a moth. Far out! I wonder how much of it is thanks to the Tinkers. Or are there entire planets of rock people?

"I guess I wouldn't mind watching Sirra get pulverized," I say, turning back to Nola. "What is it, some kind of training machine?"

"More like a game. People play one another to see who can stay in longest. I once pawned off a whole week's bilge-cleaning duty to Jom on a bet that Ghost would beat Etander. And it's fun. Sirra won't get pulverized, though. She's too good. Watch."

Sirra cartwheels over two smashing metal plates and hangs in midair for a long moment, arms flung out artistically. Even with a giant deathtrap trying to take her out, she's going for the glamour shots. I'm kind of impressed, in spite of myself.

The lights in the Arena abruptly switch from orange to blue. The flames wink out. Sirra flips down to land triumphantly outside the Arena.

"She's good, isn't she?" says Nola, sounding wistful. "You could totally take her, with your Tech mojo."

"Oh, they'd call it cheating."

"She's using her superpowers. Who says you can't?"

Nola ducks her head. "I couldn't go in there, anyway. It's too dangerous. Look." She points at a dial on the side of the ring. "That was only level five, and did you see those fire jets?" She shudders.

"Eh, it doesn't look too hard."

Me and my big mouth. My words ring out into one of those weird lulls in the conversations around us. Every single person hears me. And stares.

"Hey, everybody," says Nola, doing her best to cover for me. "This is Trix. She's new. Trix, this is . . . uh . . . everybody!"

"Not too hard, is it?" Sirra bounds down from the platform, arms crossed, chin high. "I'd like to see you last three minutes, Earth Girl."

No backing down now. "Sure. But only if we make it interesting."

"Interesting?"

I march over to the panel and spin the dial as high as it goes. Excitement buzzes through the crowd. Sirra's eyes go wide.

"Trix!" says Nola. "Are you sure? Level thirteen?"

"It's okay. I know what I'm doing." I lower my voice. "If we stick to the easy stuff and Sirra beats me, I'll look like an idiot. Even Sirra is scared of level thirteen."

"And what about you?"

I try to smile. "I'm more scared of looking stupid."

"Sirra, don't," says a boy with the same coppery skin and slippery dark hair as Sirra. "You don't need to prove—"

"I do, Etander. Someone needs to show the new girl how things work around here. She obviously doesn't know her place. She probably can't even do a cartwheel."

I say nothing. Instead I try to shake out some of the tension from my arms, roll my neck, and wiggle my toes.

"Trix," whispers Nola, "don't do it!"

I'm already moving, taking the three bounding steps that propel me into a front handspring, step out, round-off, back handspring. As I slam down from my double twisting layout onto the edge of the Arena, the crowd erupts in whoops of surprise. I wink at Sirra. "Ready when you are, Sparkles."

Sirra grimaces, then vaults over the steps, pulling a midair somersault to land on her hands beside me. Supporting herself one-armed, she waves. The onlookers cheer even louder.

"Watch out in there," says Sirra, bobbing upright. "This is no place for newbies."

"How's your nose?" I don't wait to see her reaction. It's time to face the Arena.

Someone, probably Nola, shouts, "Go, Trix!"

As soon as my feet touch the floor, about five billion things start trying to kill me. I duck under a giant rolling pin studded with jabby spikes. I twist out of the way of shooting flames. I leap up to grab a dangling hook, narrowly avoiding a pit that falls away under my feet. It's taking all my energy just to stay in the game. I've got to focus. I only need to last three minutes.

It feels like it's been an hour already. Sweat streams down my neck, tickling my skin. I throw myself under another swipe of the giant rolling pin. I may not be posing, but I'm surviving.

Then the net gets me.

Threads of fire burn through my body. It catches me by the legs and one arm. It's going to toss me out. I claw with my free hand for anything that can keep me inside the Arena.

My slippery fingers scrabble against smooth metal, then catch. I grit my teeth against the crackling pain that pulses from the net. I'm holding one of the spikes that pokes up from the floor. All I want is to let go and escape the pain, but I can't. I won't give up.

"You'll never make it, Earth Girl!" Sirra pirouettes aside, evading a blast of flame. "Let go!"

"Make me."

"Fine. If that's what it takes." Sirra leaps, soaring over the intervening obstacles to thump down in front of me. "What do you think of the Arena now?" Her eyes glitter with the reflected blue sparks popping off the net.

"Not . . . so tough," I huff. "Might . . . take . . . a

nap." I force a grin. I can tell her patience is running out. I only need her to come a little bit closer.

Sirra snarls, reaching for my fingers. Before she can wrench them free, I let go and grab her instead. She shrieks and kicks, but I've got a good grip. I hold tight as the net flips me up into the air, so that we both go flying out of the Arena. We slam to the ground in a tangled heap.

Sirra throws herself off me, planting an elbow in my gut along the way. I don't care. I made it a tie. That's good enough.

The translator can't handle whatever it is Sirra's saying as she stalks off, but I get the picture. I start to laugh, but it hurts.

"Trix!" cries Nola, popping up over my head. "You were amazing!"

I manage a smile, barely. All I want is to lie there for a few years enjoying my victory and waiting for my body to feel less like a sack of jelly.

A weird wailing echoes from the ceiling. All at once everybody's moving, heading for doors and chattering.

"Trix?" Nola asks. "Are you all right?"

I shake myself. "Considering that the day started with my hair turning pink and ended on a circus space-ship filled with mutant outlaws, yeah, I'm surprisingly all right."

"Come on, then. Let's check out your new home."

My new home.

CHAPTER 6

Breakfast of Champions

THE NEXT MORNING I'm still tucked into my bed yawning as Nola bops around showing off the different gadgets she's installed "for fun." She tried giving me the rundown last night, but I was so wiped I fell asleep pretty much as soon as she popped down my foldaway bed. I'm still not entirely sure this isn't all a crazy dream, except that if it were, the dorm would probably be bigger. It's actually smaller than my room at Bleeker, but about a million times more comfy.

The walls are chock-full of all kinds of stuff. A woman

sitting on a giant thresher waves from one picture. It could be a cornfield in Iowa, except there are two moons in the sky. One whole wall is filled with engineering schematics. And there's a pair of impossibly beautiful identical women gazing smolderingly from a poster right beside Nola's bed. I can't read the alien script above them, but I'm pretty sure it says *Love Among the Stars*.

"And see this?" Nola gives her desk a push. It flips up, disappearing into the wall. "All the furniture is foldaway. Oh, and check this out." She presses her palm to the wall. It changes color, from green to bright pink.

"To match your hair," Nola says. "Or try this." The walls go dark, speckled with stars. "It's what you'd see if we were outside. The program patches in from the external sensors, so it's all live feed. It took me three days to work out how to integrate them, but isn't it neat?"

"Whoa!" I pull myself out of bed to spin around, taking it all in. "You even did the floor." Stars drift below my feet. It's kind of freaky, but amazing.

"So you like it? You think you'll be okay here? I mean, rooming here?"

"Absolutely. Who wouldn't be? I've got supergenius Tech Girl to show me the ropes and the cushiest bed in the galaxy."

But as I stare out into the limitless expanse, I can't help shivering. Nyl is out there, somewhere, waiting to get his hands on my meteorite. What if he finds us? Just how safe is my fabulous new life?

"What?" Nola glances around. "Is it making you space-sick?"

I shake off my fears. There's no reason to worry Nola. Nyl's probably light-years away. "No. It's great. So where do we get breakfast? I'm starved. Please tell me you don't live on weird energy drinks and protein pills."

"Oh, no—the food here is amazing! Jom isn't even a Tech, but he's got the culinary protocols figured out better than any of us, what with the family business and all that. You just have to be careful with his experiments . . ."

Nola trails off, her eyes wandering. She cocks her head, raising one hand to her know-it-all. She nods, then says, "Got it, Miss Three. I'll be there quick as I can. I need to drop Trix off for breakfast." Her conversation apparently finished, she looks at me, a hint of worry in her eyes.

"What's up?"

"I need to help with the test setup. They want to run you through after breakfast, to find out what you can do. Don't worry; you'll be fine."

A pang of fear twists my stomach. Breakfast suddenly sounds a lot less appealing. "Sounds like fun. Can't wait."

My insides don't quiet down, even with the distraction of Nola showing me the bathrooms, the storage lockers, and the laundry chute. By the time we reach the cafeteria, I feel like a pair of boa constrictors is having a fight in my stomach.

The rest of the troupe crowds around four of the tables, helping themselves from the army of steaming platters. There's a fifth table standing lonely in the corner, completely empty. Yeah, that's a good sign. Social failure, here I come.

"I'm sorry," Nola says, twisting her hands together. "I feel horrible setting you loose in the cafeteria by yourself."

"Are you worried about me or the rest of the troupe?" I say, smiling so maybe she won't see how nervous I am.

"Heh. Maybe both. But seriously, you'll be fine. You could sit with the Techs. They wouldn't mind."

"Yeah." I follow her gesture to the seven kids at the nearest table. "I don't think they'd even realize I was there." Every one of them has a sparky wrench insignia and is wearing what look like large wraparound sunglasses. They sit staring straight ahead, eating in complete silence.

Nola winces. "It's easier to talk and eat at the same time if you do the talking virtually. No choking."

"Smart. It's okay; I can handle this. Go on. I'll see you later."

Nola still looks worried, but she nods. "You really

better turn on your know-it-all, Trix. You'll need it to find the testing room."

"Okay, okay. After breakfast. I'm not eating with that thing babbling in my ear about evil twins from some silly soap opera."

I watch Nola head off, glad for an excuse to keep my back to the room while I come up with a plan of attack. I'll turn around, walk past each of the tables, and see if anyone looks friendly. If they completely ignore me, I'll sit at the empty one and make it my own.

I really hope they don't ignore me. Please let just one person give me a smile. Even a smirk! I can work with a smirk. All right. Here I go. I straighten my shoulders and turn around.

The Techs are a lost cause, so I move on to the next table, where a dozen or so boys and girls lounge like a pack of lions in the sun. Stars glitter from the patches decorating their jackets, shirts, and scarves. Sirra doesn't ignore me, that's for sure, but her look hardly says "Come sit at my table and we'll make up." It's more like "Get out of my spaceship and never come back." I keep walking.

The third table is the smallest, and the collection of people around it is definitely the oddest. A boy who looks a lot like a giant snail sits snuffling a plate of spongy brown cutlets. He's flanked by the rock boy I saw last night and a kid who looks like a walking alligator. The most normal of the group is a girl with a crackling haystack of white-blond hair who stares at me through thick, dark-rimmed goggles.

I guess I better give it a shot.

"Hey," I say. "I'm new here. My name's Trix."

The blonde tilts her head. "One thousand three hundred forty-nine. Go and find it. Go!"

I back away. "Ahhh. Okay. Table's full. Got it." Great. Even the Freaks don't want me. One more left before I'm doomed to the Siberia of table five.

I can't see much of the fourth table, because there are about twenty kids packed around it. Popcorn Boy is there, with his cockatoo crest of red hair. He's balancing three knives end to end as he tilts back in his chair. A girl with curly green hair sits perched on the back of her own seat, juggling what look like blueberry muffins. As I watch, she bounces one in a very unmuffinlike way off the table. The only person who isn't joking, juggling, laughing, or dancing is the girl in black at the very end of the table, who's completely ignoring the rest of them.

"Hey, Theon, do you like my new act?" asks Popcorn Boy as he adds a fourth knife to his tower.

"You call balancing a few knives an act?" says the green-haired girl. "Give it up, Jom. And while you're at it, try not to rubberize the muffins next time."

"They taste fine. Besides, this way no one will notice if you drop one." He gives her a cheeky grin.

"You are so going to regret that." The girl, Theon,

71 ✡

begins pelting the redhead with her muffins. He yelps and topples backward.

Everyone ducks as the cutlery goes flying, except the goth chick at the end of the table. She just looks bored, even with one of the knives flying right into her forehead. No, *through* her forehead! Like she's a ghost or something! Unbelievable! The knife clatters onto the floor behind her. She picks up one of the muffins, dusts it off, and takes a bite.

This is *definitely* where I belong.

I run through possible lines. *Hi, I'm Trix. Please let me sit with you so I don't look like a dork.* No, definitely not. *Hi, I'm Trix. I've got no idea what I can do, but you guys look like the most fun bunch, so here I am.* I sigh. It might work.

I'm about to try it out when someone taps my shoulder. It's the boy who tried to call Sirra off last night. "Hi," he says, smiling. And it's an honest-to-goodness smile, too. "Do you need a place to sit?"

I shoot one look at the empty fifth table. "Um. Yeah. Guess it's a little obvious I'm new here. Trix. Is my name, I mean. Beatrix Ling. But you can call me Trix." Man, could I sound *any* dorkier?

"I'm Etander. Come on, you can sit with us." He starts back toward the Principals' table. Okay, I can do this. I slide into the chair Etander offers and hope I'm not smiling like a maniac as he introduces me to the Principals.

I'm sure my know-it-all would be happy to record

their names, but I am *not* ready to deal with that level of crazy right now. Within five minutes about the only thing I can remember is that the black and white spotted girl who bends light is named Dalmatian, and she only joined the troupe a few months ago herself. The others are a mixture of flashy outfits and exotic colors who do things like contortion and tightrope balancing and sound sculpture, whatever that is.

"And you already met my sister, Sirra Centaurus," Etander finishes.

Sirra looks like she's sucking on a lemon. "This is the Principals' table, Etander. Not a home for strays."

"Don't mind her," says Etander, rolling his eyes. "She's not used to anyone matching her in the Arena. You did very well."

"Not as well as your sister," I answer, feeling generous now that I have potential allies. "So does that mean you're from the Centaurus galaxy cluster?"

Etander clears his throat, glancing at Sirra. "Yes."

"Ignore the humble act," says someone at the end of the table. "It means their family *owns* it."

"The Centaurus Corporation owns it," snaps Sirra. "And we're here now, like it or not. So it doesn't matter. Drop it. We're neglecting our guest of honor." She pushes a platter of bright yellow curds across the table. "Try the scrambled pepper-eggs, Trix. They're delicious."

"You ought to check with your know-it-all," says Etander. "It might not be safe."

"Oh, I'm sure Trix is up for anything." Sirra smiles. "She did match me in the Arena."

"Yeah, but I'm not stupid." I tap the button on my earpiece. Nothing. "Um. Know-it-all? Are you there?"

"Oh, so we're talking again, are we? You invite me in and then you shut me out. Don't you care about *my* feelings?"

"Not really," I say. "Are pepper-eggs safe to eat?"

My know-it-all huffs. "For that, my dear, I very well might keep the latest *Love Among the Stars* scoop to myself."

"Good. I've heard enough about that stupid show already. Just tell me if I can eat the eggs."

"Are you sure? It's quite the shocker! Oooh, the plot twists!"

"Just. Yes. Or. No."

"Yes." My know-it-all goes silent. If it had a body, I bet it would be crossing its arms and looking pointedly away. I flop a spoonful of the eggs onto my empty plate. My stomach grumbles. I hope they taste as good as they smell.

I pause, fork raised partway to my lips. Sirra is giving me an awfully strange look. I wonder if she's planning to wig me out by telling me these are bug eggs or something. But I've already seen half the other kids eating them. And my know-it-all said they were safe. I take a bite.

My mouth bursts into flames. Seriously, it feels like

someone is rubbing hot coals along my tongue. I sputter, forcing myself to gulp down the bite rather than risk spewing it on everyone else. Not that Sirra doesn't deserve it.

"Little spicy?" Sirra asks, taking a bite of her own, hoity-toity as a lady eating tea sandwiches.

I try to say something rude, but it hurts too much. I grab a glass of green juice and suck it down so fast I don't even taste it. Maybe the pepper-eggs already burned away my taste buds.

"Mmmphhhagh! Stupid overgrown encyclopedia!" I slap my earpiece. "What was that, Britannica? You said they were safe!"

"They are," chirps the know-it-all, rather smugly. "You're alive."

"Why didn't you *warn* me it was going to burn my mouth out?"

"Yes or no. I believe those were your exact words."

I fume incoherently. It doesn't help that half the table is giggling. No way. Not here. Not again. I will *not* be the loser everyone else laughs at.

"Come on," says Sirra, rising. "Time for those of us who belong here to get to work. Miss Three is waiting for us."

The rest of the table filters away, leaving me rubbing my streaming eyes. As I'm fumbling for more juice, someone pushes something crusty and crumbly into my hand.

"Eat that," says Etander. "It should cut the heat. According to my know-it-all, that is."

I blink at the thing in my hand. It looks like a piece of toast. I figure things can't really get much worse, so I take a bite. It doesn't make everything magically all better, but he's right: It does dull the pain. I look up to thank Etander, but he's gone already, disappearing out the door with his sister.

"Listen up, you demonic thing," I inform my know-it-all. "You are going to take me to Nola. You are not leaving out any more important details. You are not letting me make a fool of myself."

"I'm a know-it-all, dear, not a miracle worker."

"I mean it. Or I'm cutting your feed from *Love Among the Stars*."

"You wouldn't *dare!*"

"Try me."

"Hmmph. Very well. Stand up from the table. Turn left. Walk twenty paces. Go through the door. Turn right—"

"You're pushing it, Britannica."

"They *are* important details."

I groan. "After this, being tested for superpowers'll be a picnic." I stand up, turn left, and walk twenty paces out the door.

CHAPTER 7

Placement

SO WHO'S MISS THREE?" I ask as I do yet
another lap around the common room, too nervous to sit.
I feel like a pinball, rattling around waiting to be bounced
in or out of the game. "I thought she was training the
Principals right now."

"She is," says Nola. She sits cross-legged on the floor,
fiddling with a bundle of blinking wires and mechanical
guts that hang from the wall. "She's an artificial intelli-
gence, but she's got three different simulacra. Did that
translate? You know what I'm talking about, right?"

I stop pacing. "In the movies on Earth, the AIs are usually the bad guys."

"Well . . ." Nola twiddles with one of the wires, zapping it with her wrench.

"I don't like the sound of that."

"She *is* a bad guy. Was, I mean. She was created by the Mandate, years and years ago."

"And you invited her onto your Tinker ship? I thought the Mandate were the Big Bad?"

"The Ringmaster reprogrammed Miss Three himself. He wanted to learn about the Mandate, and Miss Three can teach us."

"So you can fight them?"

"You cannot fight the Mandate," says a voice that bites my skin like a static shock. I whirl around to see a ghostly figure in a dark suit that definitely was not there a moment ago. The hologram holds a clipboard and stylus as insubstantial as herself. With her slicked-back hair and perfect bone structure, she reminds me a lot of a department store mannequin.

Nola stops fiddling with her wires and scrambles to her feet. "Miss Three, this is—"

"Our beloved Ringmaster's newest recruit. Beatrix Ling. Lately of Sol-3, commonly called Earth by the distressing melange of individuals that live there," says Miss Three. "Currently unclassified."

I straighten my shoulders. "I'm ready for your tests."

"Convinced you're something special, are you? No doubt he's already filled your head with dreams of being a star."

I stare right back. No way some microchip is getting me riled up.

She gives a little shrug, then runs a stylus across her clipboard. "Let's get started, then. We'll begin with the medical examination."

An hour later, I've been poked and pricked and prodded enough for a hundred checkups. I lift weights, run on a treadmill, jump, tumble, balance, and throw darts at a screen. All the while Miss Three watches, like it's all some faintly amusing practical joke.

Nola hustles around silently, fetching this or that instrument when Miss Three requests it, occasionally shooting me reassuring looks.

I'm trying harder than I've tried for anything in my whole life. I know I nail the physical tests. But I don't warp gravity. I don't shoot lightning out of my fingertips. Aside from my pink hair, I'm depressingly normal.

"That's enough, Nola," says Miss Three. "Clearly Miss Ling has only an average degree of visual recall."

Nola gulps and flicks a switch. The shapes vanish from the wallscreen.

"Wait! Let me try again! I *do* have a good memory. I've got practically every constellation memorized."

"All well and good, Miss Ling, but I'm afraid our

audiences are unlikely to be entertained by a recitation of crude astronomical nomenclature pertaining to a sky they will never see."

"But Miss Three, there are still other—" begins Nola.

"No. It's clear to me you have no extraordinary abilities. There is no need to resort to extreme measures. Now you see how empty the Ringmaster's promises are." She gives me a plastic smile. "Not everyone can be a star. I regret that he has raised such false hopes, but it is better to learn the truth now, while you can still return to some sort of reasonable life."

I am *not* settling for some secondhand clunker of a life when I can get the newest, snazziest model. "Hang on a minute. Why isn't the Ringmaster here? Maybe he ought to judge for himself what I can do. He's the one who asked me to stay."

"The Ringmaster is a busy man and does not have time for trivialities."

"This is my future we're talking about. It's not trivial to *me*." I flick my know-it-all. "Hey, Britannica, get the Ringmaster on the line, will you? Tell him Beatrix is getting fed up with these stupid tests."

"So sorry, dear, the Ringmaster is unavailable right now. Would you like to hear his away message? It's *so* amusing. Though not as amusing as what Dalana says when the space pirate Zendalos surprises her in—"

I grit my teeth and switch it off. Miss Three raises her brow in an arch so perfect it looks like it was drawn with a protractor.

I turn to Nola. "You said there are more tests."

"Yes, but Trix, they're dangerous! Maybe we should wait—"

"I want to get this over with. Got that?" I say to Miss Three.

"If you are willing to risk so much in this foolish quest, then by all means, proceed."

"Do it."

Nola nods and lays her silver hand against the wall. In the middle of the room, the Arena springs to life with a wheeze of grinding metal. The dial on the panel is gone, replaced by a single flashing purple word: OVERRIDE.

"What do I have to do?"

"Step inside," says Miss Three. "And survive."

I strip off my jacket, feeling the heavy lump of the meteorite in one pocket. What if Nyl was telling the truth? Maybe I'm not really Tinker-touched, just a normal Earth girl jazzed up by a space rock. Miss Three seems to think I'm nothing special.

With my back to the others, I close my eyes for a moment. No. My parents promised. And I got through that door. That must count for something. Come on, Tinkers. You must have given me more than pink hair.

I'll take anything. Gravity, fire. Okay, maybe not a snail shell. But let me stay here. Let me be something more.

I step into the Arena. The ground disappears. I fall, twisting aside in time to avoid being skewered by spikes lining the pit.

If I thought last night was bad, this is a million times worse. I dive and jump, my legs and arms already weak from all the other tests. I'm too slow. I'm not going to make it. Miss Three is right. I'm an idiot.

Faint bluish light haloes the mallets and spikes and every other instrument of death racing to take me out. I'm shaking; it's not only fear and complete exhaustion. Energy jolts my bones. The whole Arena hums with power. My hair's in my eyes. I try to brush it back, but it sticks to my fingers, crackling with static. A jolt of pure agony spills me onto the floor. I scream. My hands feel like I've dunked them in acid. Nola's voice echoes dimly through a fog of pain.

"Miss Three, we've got to stop it!"

"You heard Miss Ling, Nola. She asked for this."

I open my lips to scream, but nothing comes out. All I have is pain.

It stops. For a brief and glorious moment I think it's me, that I've found some Tinker-power to switch off the light show. Then I open my eyes and see him.

"Ringmaster. I didn't . . . I was trying . . ." The words choke me. I don't want it to be real. I've failed. One day, and I've already trashed the biggest dream of my entire life. I don't belong here.

"I understand," he says, holding out a hand to help me up off the floor. "But I think that's quite enough for now."

"Ringmaster," says Miss Three, "you should know that this was all at her own request. She understood the consequences and insisted that we proceed. It is unfortunate that such extreme measures were necessary to convince her of her lack of—"

"Thank you, Miss Three, Nola. I'd like to have a word with Beatrix now."

Miss Three's simulacrum winks out, her taunting smile lingering in a ghost of photons. Nola starts packing up her tools, moving about as slow as molasses. She gives me an encouraging nod, but there's a worried crinkle between her eyes. I try to smile back. Then finally she snaps the toolbox closed. The door shuts behind her, and I'm alone with the Ringmaster.

I stand miserably, trembling all over from the aftereffects of the test and the fear of what he's about to say.

"So, would you prefer nachos or cake?"

"What?"

"Ah, you're quite right. Why choose? We'll have both. Excellent!"

I stare at him, wondering if one of the aftereffects of my thrashing is hallucinations.

"For brunch," he says. "Another fabulous word: *brunch*. Not quite one thing or the other, but sometimes it's exactly what you need. Come along." He sets off briskly toward the door. "There's something I'd like you to see, so you can begin to understand."

"Understand what?"

The Ringmaster spins around, arms flung wide. "All of this. The Big Top, the rest of the troupe, the show itself."

"But I don't have any superpowers. Aren't you going to kick me out?" My voice cracks.

"I didn't travel three hundred parsecs to Earth just for the avocados."

"You really mean it?" I'm going to cry at any moment, but I've got to say it. "You're not sending me away? I mean, it's crazy, I know, but . . ." I squeeze my eyes shut on the tears and whisper, "I'd die if I had to go back."

Cool fingers touch my cheek, making me jump. "Beatrix, I swear to you on . . . on the honor of my name, I will never, ever ask you to leave the Big Top. This is your home now. Please believe that."

My shudder of relief nearly topples me. The Ringmaster's hand slips lower, catching me around the shoulders. "I'm not sure which of us is a bigger fool. You, for nearly killing yourself trying to prove you belong. Or me, for not expecting you'd do that." He gives me an inscrutable look.

"I'm sorry I can't do anything," I say when I find my voice again. "All I have is this stupid pink hair."

"Pink is an underrated color," he says. "Some of the best things in the universe are pink. Sunrises. Erasers. Flamingos. And . . . well, there are those shellfish you can get potted with brown butter."

"Thanks. I feel so much better knowing I remind you of a prawn."

He grins. "That sense of humor will serve you better than any Tinker power. Now, can you walk? Good. Follow me."

We travel along several corridors, then down something like a firefighter's pole that puffs out a cushion of air at the bottom. I walk out into a room that definitely does not belong on a spaceship.

Gilt-framed paintings and old-fashioned green lamps fill the few bits of wall that aren't crammed floor to ceiling with bookshelves. A bunch of study carrels fills the far end. I see the blonde from breakfast in one of them. She doesn't even look up when we come in. Her carrel is filled with a dozen video screens, each of them playing something different. There's no one else in the room.

"The library," the Ringmaster announces.

"We're eating in the library?"

"Don't tell Miss Three. She'd like to have a rule against eating anywhere outside the cafeteria. But I defy anyone to read the picnic scene in *Moons over Mizzebar* without a snack. It's impossible."

"You brought me here to read about a picnic?"

"It's a brilliant book, picnics aside," he says. "But we're here for something else." He leads the way to a low table bearing matched silver-domed platters. As I sink into one of the pudgy armchairs, he pulls the covers away with a flourish.

Two heaping servings of nachos lie drenched in cheese and salsa and beans, sprinkled with black olives, and decorated with giant dollops of guacamole. The cake stands proudly alongside, topped with candied pineapple and ruby-red cherries, oozing caramel.

"Help yourself. I've got to find something."

He doesn't need to tell me twice. Now that the terrible knots are starting to unwind, I'm starving. As I chow down, the Ringmaster flits along the shelves, muttering and occasionally resting a hand on a volume, only to pull away.

"Aha! *A Treatise on the Social Conventions, Taboos, and Millinery of Deneb-5*. Perfect!"

"You want me to read about hats?" I ask around a mouthful of cheese and beans.

"What? No, the book's rubbish," he says as he returns to the table. "Miss Three insisted I read it before our last—and consequently only—performance on Deneb-5. But it's perfect raw material for the replicator."

I watch in alarm and fascination as he piles a mountain of avocado and beans onto a chip, all while balancing the book atop his baton, defying both gravity and common sense. Maybe that's his superpower. That and the ability to wear a bazillion sequins without looking like an ass.

After piloting the loaded chip into his mouth, the Ringmaster heads for the nearest painting. The stern lady in the portrait disappears, to be replaced by a slot like a library book drop and a glowing screen. The Ringmaster pops his book into the slot, then taps the screen. A loud whirring and clacking echoes from beyond the wall. With a triumphant trill of beeps, a dark oblong pops out. The Ringmaster stares at the cover for a long moment.

"Didn't it come out right?"

He sighs, so faintly I almost think I'm imagining it. "No, it's fine." He hands me the book, then plops down and begins polishing off the rest of his nachos.

I can barely make out the title. *The Programme of the Circus Galacticus, Twelfth Edition.* Someone used up an entire lifetime supply of gold curlicues decorating this thing. I flip to a random page and read aloud. " 'Act Nine: Firedance. Having gained the Seeds of the Tree of Life, the Dreamers seek to Kindle the Seeds in the Fires of the King. As the Trickster confuses and beguiles the King, the Dreamers carry out a series of foudroyant escapades . . . ' " I look up. "Is *foudroyant* a real word or is the translator being goofy?"

"It's most certainly a real word, and an excellent one at that. It means *dazzling.*"

"And you didn't think it might be easier just to say *dazzling*?"

"You can never have too many words that mean *dazzling*. Besides, I didn't write it. The Big Top did."

"The spaceship takes notes on your performances?"

"The Big Top is more than a spaceship. And it's not notes; it's a script. A performance by the Circus Galacticus is more than death-defying feats and amusements. It's a story."

"Like a musical, but with clowns and acrobatics?"

He taps his nose. "Exactly."

"Do you mean the Big Top writes the plot? Is it always the same?"

"Yes and no," replies the Ringmaster vaguely as he carves off a chunk of cake and wraps it in a napkin. I crunch down on my last handful of chips, waiting for more answers.

"But you should read *The Programme* before we continue this conversation," he says, standing. "You do that, and I'll be back before you miss me." He winks, toasting me with his slice of cake, then disappears out the door before I can do more than sputter through my mouthful of corn chips.

The blonde is watching me. "You don't fit," she says. "You have to find it."

"Um. Okay." I slouch down, open *The Programme* to page one, and begin reading.

It starts with a cast list of a dozen characters. First up is "The Ringmaster: Madcap and Mysterious, he awakens Dream and Color in the grim world of the sleepers held fast within the hold of the Iron King."

I read through the rest of them, my brain struggling under the onslaught of melodramatic word choices and capital letters. Some of the entries don't make a lot of sense. There's one for a character called the Trickster: "Veiled in Shadow, he may be Friend or Foe." I've got no clue who that is.

Others are clear enough. "The Stardancer: A Graceful Voyager who cavorts among the Stars, her Beauty and Power inspire the Dreamers to hold fast to their Hope." Sirra's got beauty and power all right, but what she inspires in me isn't hope. More like loathing.

The last entry is for "The Lightbearer: Dappled in Light and Dark, she Illuminates the Treachery of the King." That must be Dalmatian, with her spotted skin and light-bending powers.

It goes on into descriptions of each act. I skim the entire book pretty quickly. By the time the Ringmaster comes back, I'm rereading the last few acts.

He's changed his coat to a blindingly lime-green version, and there's something that resembles a singed bullet hole in the crown of his top hat. But he slides gracefully into his chair with the air of someone who's just taken a refreshing stroll in the park.

"So?" he asks. "What do you think?"

"It's sort of like a fairy tale or something. But it's— sorry—a little weird."

The Ringmaster nods and mm-hmms in a way that doesn't tell me anything useful, so I continue. "These Dreamer people want to reach the stars, so they try a bunch of different things. But the King and his Minions stop them every time, and then finally the Oracle tells them to go to the Tree of Life. So they go and—is there *really* an act that involves dancing fruit?"

"It's quite a crowd pleaser, actually," says the Ring-master.

"If you say so. Anyway, they get the magic beans. But for some reason, they need to dunk them in the King's fires to make them grow, so the Trickster helps them do that. And then he disappears, and so does the King, and everyone lives happily ever after, which makes no sense."

He leans forward, drumming his fingers against the jeweled top of his baton. "Why?"

"There's something missing."

"Ah." He leans back again, looking remarkably pleased with himself. "I knew you were clever. Please, elucidate."

"Well, for one, the Iron King fellow causes all this trouble and then what? He just goes away and lets them fly up into the stars at the end? There ought to be a big fight or something. And the description of the Light-bearer talks about her revealing treachery, but that never happens." I thump the book down on the table. "Why are there twelve editions? There's something you're not explaining."

"Many things, in point of fact," says the Ringmaster. "Infuriating, isn't it? But if I sent you to the corner market to buy bread, you'd go straight to the bakery section, pick up your loaf, and be off. There might be perfectly ripe tomatoes and cans of curried sardines, and you'd walk right on by without even taking notice."

"If I saw curried sardines, I'd *definitely* keep walking," I say. "And what if you really needed bread?"

"The point is, most people become blind if they're told what to do."

"Are you going to explain about the twelve editions or not?"

"Twelve editions," echoes a clear, sharp voice from across the room. It's the blonde. "Twelve characters."

"Oh, now, that's cheating," protests the Ringmaster, but I'm already opening the book to the front and peering at the cast list.

"She's right. There are twelve of them." I tap my finger under the last entry. "The Lightbearer is Dalmatian. And she was the last one to join, before me. So the Big Top creates a new *Programme* whenever a new person comes on board? No, that can't be right, because there's more than twelve of us. What? Why are you smiling like that?"

"You said 'us.'"

"Maybe I shouldn't have. I'm not in *The Programme*."

"Not every new member of the troupe produces a new edition of *The Programme*."

"But you thought I might." Now I understand that look he'd had, earlier, staring at the book. My insides sink, dragging me deeper into the chair.

"Chin up, Beatrix. You'll make a brilliant Clown, for the time being."

"For the time being?"

"Until something changes. No, don't ask. Remember the sardines."

"I don't understand, though, why you bother calling people Clowns and Principals and Freaks. They're all in here in *The Programme,* one way or another."

He pauses, like he's not sure which answer to give me. Finally he says, "Those labels—they're meant to help you work together, not to divide you."

"Hmph. Tell that to Sirra."

He raises an eyebrow. "None of us is perfect, Beatrix. Everyone here deserves to be given a chance, including Sirra. You're not the only one I invited onto this ship."

What? He's taking *Sirra's* side? Has he not been paying attention?

"So you're okay with it all? You like having everyone sitting at their own special table?"

"Of course I don't like it," says the Ringmaster sharply.

"Then do something about it! Can't you make them—"

"No!" The bullet-crack violence of the word sends me cringing back in my seat. "It doesn't work that way. That's what *they* do. It's not why I'm here." The Ring-master is on his feet, hands clenched to white knuckles on his baton, all trace of the lighthearted jester snuffed out.

My mouth is dry, but I force a question out, to release the painful tension that fills the air. "Then why *are* you here?"

Something seems to break in his eyes, and he sinks back into his chair, the baton now loose in his hands, resting across his sharp knees. He laughs, but there's a bitterness to it. "That, Beatrix, is an exceptionally good question. And I'll give you one in return. How do you free someone when he doesn't even realize he's in a cage? Sometimes we like our prisons. They can be very comfortable. What would you do?"

"I'd bust them all. Every one."

"Somehow I believe you could do it," he says, smiling for real. He springs lightly to his feet and pulls me to join him. "Enough philosophizing. It's time for the Clowns' afternoon training session. Let's go and show them how *foudroyant* you can be."

CHAPTER 8

Firedance

APPARENTLY even on a spaceship the size of the Big Top there aren't a lot of open areas, so we head to the main performance ring for the practice session. It's a little different than I remember it. The "tent" walls still swoop up into dark heights, but most of the bleachers are collapsed into heaps of metal along the sides.

There are other differences: Bottles of water and shoes lie in scattered heaps outside the Ring. The lights are steady and bright, and the soundtrack is the drumming of feet and the counts and calls of the performers. The fantastic costumes and makeup are gone.

And it is *still* damn impressive. I hang back by the doors. Am I crazy? Can I really do this?

The Ringmaster turns to me. "Nervous?"

"No! I mean, yeah, a little. It's just . . . I don't know the routines." And they might all hate me.

"Never fear. You'll shine."

"Yeah, I can see it now. A big, shiny fall on my ass."

He laughs, which somehow makes it better. "We all fall sometimes. I once tripped clear out of the Ring right in the middle of the grand finale. Ended up in the lap of the ambassador from the Thenx Syndicate. Nothing can be as bad as that, believe me."

"Why? Was the ambassador upset?"

"No. She wouldn't let me go! Kept shoving universal credit chits down my shirt front."

"That doesn't sound so—"

"With her tentacles."

"Okay, okay, you win." I take a breath and raise one hand to the Clown insignia newly clipped onto my jacket. "Let's do this."

Now it's the Ringmaster's turn to hesitate, like an actor about to step onstage. He closes his eyes, just for a moment. It's funny, he's so effortlessly dazzling—so *foudroyant*—but how much wattage does it take to keep that charm blazing? What happens when the batteries need recharging?

I'm about to ask if he's okay, but by the time I open my mouth, he's plunging ahead into the room. The moment he steps into the Ring, every eye is on him. Seriously, I even check up top for a spotlight, but there's nothing. It's all him. The Clowns break off their practice and surge toward us in a mob.

"Hello, hello, my jongleurs and jollies," he calls out as the tide of performers crashes into him, then breaks apart to surround us in an excited and slightly sweaty pool. "Practice goes smashingly as ever, I see. Theon, that last leap was excellent. You'll have the crowd on its feet."

At this, the green-haired girl who was juggling muffins at breakfast grins. Another girl gives her a high-five. Her smile fades quickly, though. "They'll be on their feet walking out if we don't fix the rest of the act," she says, crossing her arms. "It's crap, Ringmaster. It doesn't work without the Trickster. And now the King's broken down again. Half the time the light and smoke don't even work. You need to do something."

"Ah, well, there are always a few hiccups, aren't there? But first, let me introduce the newest recruit to the Clown Corps. This is Beatrix Ling."

Most of them actually smile, or at least look curious. The only one who doesn't is the goth chick, but I'm guessing it would take an event bigger than me to crack a reaction out of that amount of sullen.

The green-haired girl gives me a calculating once-over, then holds out a hand. I grit my teeth and match her viselike grip. "Good, we can use some new blood. I'm Theon. I make things frictionless." Suddenly her fingers are like oil in my hand, slipping free and leaving me clutching air. "So," she says, "what can you do, Beatrix?"

"Um . . ."

"She can hold her own in the Arena, for one thing," says the boy with the brilliant red hair. "I'm Jom," he adds, giving me a wave. "Welcome to the Clown Corps, Beatrix."

"Just Trix is fine," I say. "I've got pink hair. And . . . um . . . spunk." Did I really say that? I am the definition of lameness. "But, um, I'm totally up for learning the routines. You guys look amazing out there."

"We work hard," says Theon, but she smiles, which makes her look a little less like a drill sergeant. "And don't worry; you'll catch on. You're quick. I can tell."

"Very good," says the Ringmaster. "And now . . ." He pauses, his eyes distant.

Theon groans. "Not again."

The Ringmaster comes out of the momentary daze, but he still looks distracted, like he's doing calculus in the back of his brain. "I'll be off now."

"But, Ringmaster," Theon protests, "you *promised* you'd actually stay for this practice! We wanted to show you the new bit Asha and Leri worked out. And what about the Trickster? And the King?"

"I have every confidence you can work things out, Theon. I promise I'll run through the video feeds later. But you know how these things are. We're coming up on a stellar dust field. There may be leeches. The Big Top needs me."

"So do we," mutters Theon. But he's already heading for the door. "All right, I guess we're on our own. Let's take it from the top, people. Jom, have Trix shadow you until she's got the basics."

"Don't let Theon get to you," says Jom as he leads me to the far side of the Ring. "She's got kind of an obsession with people's powers. Maybe because the best thing about hers is that she never has a bad hair day. Not that I should talk. I mean, all I do is make smells."

"Smells?"

"Yeah." He rubs a hand back across his scarlet crest of hair. "It was pretty miserable for a while. Couldn't control it. Made everything smell like rotten pepper-eggs. I think if the Ringmaster hadn't shown up, my parents were going to disown me."

"The Ringmaster helped you control your stink?"

"Yep. And now . . ."

A rich scent like the most absolutely amazingly wonderful brownie floods my nose. Seriously, I nearly fall over; it's that good. "Whoa! That's amazing. And cruel."

"Food is my forte. And don't worry; I'm doing something special for dessert tonight!" Jom winks. "Here's our starting mark," he adds, pointing out a glowing symbol on the floor.

I give a little test bounce. The entire Ring is a kind of giant trampoline. No wonder the Clowns could manage those phenomenal leaps. A little ripple of excitement fizzes through me. I can do this. It might even be fun. A bunch of other marks illuminate the floor, like a crazy-complicated set of dance steps. Jom gives me a rundown, but even so, I finally cave and flick on Britannica to help me keep track. Fortunately she seems to consider it a matter of personal honor that I nail my moves, so there's a minimum of space-opera small talk.

We run through the sequence a half-dozen times. The third time Jom has me take over his part so he can see what I make of it. After that we alternate. The translator doesn't catch everything Jom says, but it must be positive, since he's smiling. Even Theon gives me a "Nice one!" after I finally land the tricky third midair tumble without a falter. It's almost enough to bust me out of my doubts, to make me start believing the Ringmaster that this is where I belong.

As I watch the Clowns running through the Firedance for the sixth time, two things stick out. One is: These guys have some absolutely mad energy and talent. No way are they second string, even if they aren't Principals. Two is: Theon was right about the routine. It's not working.

The Programme has us Clowns divvied up, half as Dreamers, half as Minions of the Iron King. From what I remember, this act involves us trying to dunk the magic beans into the King's fire. It ends when the Trickster finally succeeds, then vanishes in a puff of smoke.

I watch the glowing dance-step symbols rippling across the stage and realize why things are so weird. There are two sets of symbols that nobody's following. When Theon calls for a rest break, Jom and I head over for a chat.

"We don't have a Trickster anymore," says Theon, popping the cap from her water bottle so hard it shoots off across the room. "And we never had any King other than old Rustbucket there." She jerks a thumb over her shoulder at the mechanical "King" at the center of the ring. I can see what she means. He's cool-looking and all, with the black spiky crown and clawlike hands. But one of his red glowing eyes is on the fritz, which makes him look like he's winking at us. And most of the time his grand gestures get stuck on repeat until someone manages to give him a thump on the back. Plus, he's supposed to be moving around, according to the choreography. I think this old guy would collapse if he tried to move an inch.

"So where are they? They're in *The Programme*."

"The way we figure it, there's never been a flesh-and-blood King," says Theon. "At least, we've been using the rustbucket since anybody can remember. But we did have a Trickster, once. He left."

"That's crazy. I mean, look at this place. Why would anybody leave?"

"I don't know the whole story," says Jom, "but the way I heard it, he ran away and joined the Outcasts."

"The what?"

"There are a lot more Tinker-touched in the universe than us," says Theon. She swigs her water, a dent deepening between her brows. "Some of them try to hide, some of them get taken by the Core or the Mandate, and some of them fight back."

"So aside from the Core Governance that wants to use us and the Mandate agents, who probably want to do something equally nasty to us, there's some sort of League of Evil Mutants out there?"

Theon nods. "I was pretty new when it all went down, but I guess Reaper thought we should be doing more, fighting the Mandate and even the Core Governance. There was a big blowup between him and the Ringmaster, and the next day he was gone. The Ringmaster never talks about it, but people say Reaper joined up with the Outcasts and—what are they doing here?"

I turn to see Sirra and Etander crossing the floor toward the Ring. Sirra steams ahead; I can almost see her flags flying for battle. Etander lags behind like an anchor trying to slow her down.

We gather into a united Clown front. Even Ghost lurks near the back of the pack. Theon is gritting her teeth, and I catch a whiff of smoke and hot metal as I take a position between her and Jom.

"We need to use the Tent," says Sirra.

"We've got another hour of practice scheduled," says Theon. "After that, it's all yours."

"We need it now."

Jom's checking something on his know-it-all. "You guys are scheduled in the small practice hall."

"The lifters broke down. Again."

"So call a Tech," says Asha, narrowing green eyes slitted like a cat's. Her twin sister nods in agreement.

"I did. But it's going to take an hour, and we need to practice."

"So do we," I say.

"That's for sure," Sirra says. "But Etander and I are Principals." I feel her eyes latching onto the Clown insignia on my collar. "People actually care about our act. The Firedance is nothing but filler now. Everyone knows it."

"Oh, really?" I cross my arms. "Want to make a bet? Our new and improved Firedance is going to blow your Skydance out of the . . . sky," I stumble over my metaphor, but I think she gets my drift.

"New Firedance?" Jom's scarlet brows arch in surprise. The hot-metal smell turns abruptly to a light peppery scent that makes my nose itch. I give him a sharp look. "Oh, right," he says. "Our new Firedance. That we've been practicing. Just now."

"I'm calling the Ringmaster," says Theon, shaking her head. "He can sort this out."

Sirra shakes her head. "There's nothing to sort out. We need the practice space."

"Sirra," says Etander, "we can wait. There's no need to—"

"Yes, there is! You know we need to work on it. You nearly missed your catch last show. We can't afford that kind of mistake!"

By this time, the rest of the Clowns are in on the action, calling out and shouting. Theon's trying to leave some kind of message for the Ringmaster. Jom is waving his hands and telling everyone to stay calm, but the cool spring rain scent he's putting out isn't settling anybody down. Even Etander's hands are shaking, though to give him credit, he still looks like he'd rather be anywhere else.

I ball my hands into fists. "You don't want this fight, Sirra. We were here first."

"You?" She laughs. "You haven't been here a week. You don't know anything about how things work around here. You're a Clown. I'm a Principal. And that's—"

"Sirra!"

Etander's choked call spins his sister around. I blink, not sure I'm seeing clearly. Something's wrong with his hands. Sharp spines pierce the skin. In a ripple of shimmering charcoal, they become something monstrous. He grimaces, lips twisting, teeth clenched. I only meet his eyes for a moment. He closes them before I have to look away from the agony and shame.

"What's wrong with him?" I ask. "Do we need to get—"

"Stay back," Sirra snaps. "He's fine!" Heedless of the spines, she takes his hands in hers. "Etander, listen to me. It's all right." She makes a gentle shushing noise, all while gripping his monstrous claws. Scarlet drips from her tight fingers to splash on the floor between them.

A growling bellow rips from Etander's twisted lips. Spines are starting to bristle along his cheeks. I flinch. Sirra doesn't. "Come back, Etander. Please." The last word is a bare whisper of desperation.

Silence holds the rest of us so tight we barely breathe as Sirra fights to pull her brother from whatever this is. The change halts, then reverses. The spines diminish. And finally Etander stands trembling and hunched, himself once more. Sirra gives a ghost of a cry and hugs him tightly, speaking too low and quick for the translator to follow.

Then, without a word or even a look, Sirra pulls Etander away, toward the exit. No one speaks until the door closes behind them.

"Okay," I say. "What was that?"

Theon clears her throat. "Etander's Tinker-touch.

Gives him a pretty rough time when it starts up. But he'll be okay."

I'm not sure what definition of okay includes turning into a monster. Poor guy. Poor Sirra. I never thought I'd be sorry for her, but I can still hear the fear in her voice. *Come back, Etander. Please.* She thought she was losing him. "Does it happen a lot? What do you do if he spikes out like that onstage?"

Jom waves a dismissive hand. "Onstage no one blinks an eye. They think it's part of the act. No more real than the Mizzebar Moon Monster."

"Hey!" says Asha. "I'll have you know our uncle has a real, live video of Mizzy. You can see her wings and everything."

Jom rolls his eyes. "Anyway, it doesn't even happen that much anymore."

"Only when he gets upset," says Theon. She scuffs a foot against the floor, looking down for a moment. When she lifts her chin, she's all business. "So what was that about a new Firedance, Trix?"

Everyone seems glad for a change of topic. Next thing I know, I've got all eyes on me. I hope I'm not about to make a huge fool of myself.

"Um . . . well, it's like you said. The routine is crap as is. Not because of you guys," I add quickly. "You're brilliant. But the missing parts are ruining it. So . . . we need to fill them in."

"You mean have one of us play the King?" Jom asks.

There's a note of excitement in his voice that tells me my crazy brainstorm might work.

"And the Trickster. We'll need to alter the choreography a little, though, since none of us can whip up shadows. So then we can do it like this." I start sketching the moves in the air with my hands, only to be met with a wall of blank looks.

"Just a moment, dear," says my know-it-all. "You look like you're swatting flies. If you'll allow me to consult with the Big Top . . . there, that's better."

More glowing symbols appear under our feet. It's the entire act, straight from *The Programme*. "Perfect! I owe you one, Britannica."

"Good," purrs the infernal device. "Then from now on we'll have no more of that particular color eye shadow. Green and pink have no business getting that near each other except on a watermelon."

I ignore the lecture and focus on my plan. "These bits will have to change," I say, pointing. Then I have my know-it-all display my alterations.

Theon shakes her head. "I don't know. *The Programme* says—"

"*The Programme* can change. Do you want us to look cool or not? Let's show them you don't need to be a Principal to get applause. Who's with me?"

Jom already has his hand raised. Then one of the cat-eyed twins, Leri, gives a shrug and raises hers. Then

Frex, the boy who can stick to walls, and then the goth-girl Ghost.

Theon is the last. "Okay. Let's do it." She punches the air and grins. "Let's show them what the Clowns can do!"

The first thing I do is call Nola. No way we're sticking with the clunky old Iron King. Nola works her magic, rejiggering the King's arms into a set of bracers that throw off fake flames. I turn these over to Jom.

"Excellent!" He backflips across the Ring and lets off a great gust of flames. "Nola, these are amazing!"

Nola beams, then tosses him the crown, which she's enhanced so that it gives off little flickers of light from the hedge of spikes that encircles it.

"Okay, so we've got a King," says Theon. "And we're set with the other changes. But what about the Trickster? Some of this stuff is pretty complicated." She taps the glowing choreography markings with her foot. "Even I would have trouble with that bit at the end. The moves are tough enough without having to worry about throwing the seeds into the flames and catching it at the end. But it's got to be spot-on, or we'll look ridiculous."

"Here, let's try it. I'll show you what I was thinking."

My snazzed-up routine isn't perfect. Theon has to tweak part of it so Asha and Leri don't slam into each other, and it takes Jom a couple of runs to get comfortable with the crown. And, yeah, I fall on my ass. Three times. The Trickster part is tough, no question. Even by the end I don't have it down, but I can feel us getting sharper. I know we can make this work.

So do the rest of the Clowns. I thought they had some crazy energy before, but that was nothing compared to this. It's like there's a current running through each of us, electrifying our lives, linking us. We are going to be freaking amazing. With enough practice.

We go late, jazzed on the joy of it all. Finally Theon calls a halt. "That's enough, guys. Good work, everyone. I think we've really got something here."

Jom claps his hands together. "All right, folks, dinner's in an hour. And in honor of our newest Clown and her brilliant new Firedance, there'll be Chocolate Supernovas all around!"

A cheer rises from the crowd. I'm buffeted by good-natured cuffs to the shoulder and slaps on the back. I promise Nola, Jom, and Theon that I'll see them in the cafeteria. "I want to run through that last move once more," I tell them.

"Don't burn out on your first day," says Theon. "Seriously, Trix. We need you to stick around. You did good today."

The glow of Theon's words takes me through another three runs. I'm too worn out for it to really help, but I can't stop. I need to do this, to make myself believe this is all real. I'm here. My crazy suggestion worked. People might even be starting to like me. I might, *finally,* belong somewhere.

By the time I'm done stretching, everyone else is gone. I'm sure my know-it-all would be happy to direct me back to the dorms, but I am so not ready for another dissection of Dalana's wardrobe. And anyway, I should be able to figure it out myself, with a little trial and error. If this really is my home now, I'd better start getting to know it. Despite one wrong turn that lands me in some kind of giant greenhouse, I get back to my room with just enough time to wash the stink off before heading to the cafeteria.

CHAPTER 9

Supernova

DINNER IS GOING MUCH BETTER than breakfast so far. The dumplings are delicious, and Nola is sitting with us at the Clown table. "What a day!" she says. "You guys are going to be amazing! When are you going to tell the Ringmaster about the changes?"

"Next time he sticks around for more than three minutes," says Theon, impaling one of her own dumplings on a chopstick, then dipping it in a bowl of dark purple sauce.

"He spent more than three minutes with Trix," says

Nola, giving me a wicked smile. "I still can't believe the Ringmaster actually invited you to have brunch with him. Alone!"

"He did leave for part of the time. And we weren't alone. That girl, the one with the glasses, she was there, too." I jerk a thumb in the direction of the Freak table.

"Good as alone, then," says Theon, "if you mean Syzygy."

"That's her name?" I wonder if the translator is working.

"A lot of us call her the Oracle," says Jom. "That's her part in the show."

"Can she really tell the future?"

"Yes," says Jom.

"No," says Theon.

"Sort of," says Nola, adding, "It's complicated. She's like a super-fast, super-powerful computer. She absorbs information and doesn't forget it, ever."

"You mean she has a photographic memory?"

"More than that. She can process it, find connections and patterns. Calculate probabilities. So it's sort of like predicting the future. In a way."

"In a freaking weird way." Theon shivers. "She once told me I'd be the last Gendari to see the Moons over Mizzebar. *And* she said I was going to—well, it was stupid. And impossible."

"Syzygy isn't bad," says Nola. "She's different, like

the rest of us. Anyway, I'd rather hear more about Trix and the Ringmaster's *private brunch*."

"There's nothing more to say." I squirm under the many eyes. "I mean, there were nachos and pineapple upside-down cake, and he showed me the *Programme*. He told me I could be a Clown. It wasn't a big deal."

From the way they're looking at me, I can see they have a different opinion. "What's his deal, anyway?" I ask. "I mean, where's he from? What's his Tinker-touch? How did he end up as Ringmaster of a mutant intergalactic circus?"

The response is a whole lot of shrugs and some off-the-wall story Asha swears is true about how the Ringmaster is secretly the long-lost son of the actress who plays Dalana on *Love Among the Stars*.

"It's just weird, don't you think?" I say. "He looks like he's twenty, tops, and acts like it, too, some of the time. And then other times . . ." I trail off, not even sure what question I'm trying to ask, or why.

Jom saves me by suddenly jumping to his feet, raising a hand to his know-it-all. "They're done! Okay folks, you know the drill: get your spoons ready!" He bounds over to the dumbwaiter.

A stir of excitement runs around the table, rippling out to the rest of the cafeteria. The Techs take off their wraparound goggles, and even the alligator boy swishes his tail and clicks his long, curved talons against the tabletop.

"Ready for what?" I grab my spoon, eyeing it dubiously.

"Jom makes the Chocolate Supernovas with paccadi nuts," says Nola. "They do fine in the oven, but when they start to cool, they get unstable. If you don't find the nut in your dish and get it out in time, it'll explode."

"Thus Chocolate Supernova," finishes Theon, twirling her spoon and grinning. "Bet I find mine first. After Ghost, of course."

I follow her look to the end of the table, where Goth Girl is in her normal spot, her chin cupped in one hand and the viewscreen of her know-it-all covering her right eye. I wonder if she's watching *Love Among the Stars.*

Jom comes back a moment later balancing five large trays—two on each arm and one on top of his head—and starts dishing out the contents. "Work quick, people!" He skids the bowls down the table into the dozens of eager hands.

"There you go," Jom says, setting the last dish in front of Nola. I can't help but notice that Nola's Supernova is about twice as big as anyone else's. The smile Jom gives her is twice as wide, too. Good for Nola. Jom seems like a nice guy. And he can cook.

Nola doesn't notice. She's busy telling me what to do. "Go on, Trix! You have to sort of bash the coating and then dig for the nut."

On my other side, Theon is already scooping out

spoonfuls of molten chocolate with a look of intense concentration. At the end of the table, Ghost reaches right into the chocolate, coming out holding a perfectly clean, acorn-shaped nut. She tosses it into the garbage chute at the center of the table and begins to eat her Supernova.

A *pong, ping, pong* of paccadi nuts rattling into the trash processor is the only noise as we all focus on defusing our desserts. The first bang makes everybody jump, but it's from down in the bowels of the trash system. More bangs follow, and I'll admit I'm starting to get nervous.

A sudden trill from the center of the cafeteria sets off a stir that has nothing to do with dessert. A screen slips down from the ceiling, filled with a Venn-like image of four interlocking rings against a gold background. "What is it?" I ask.

"A governance alert," Nola says as the screen switches to a polished woman in a dark green suit. Her plasticky voice fills the room.

"Citizens of the Core, we can now confirm reports that an uncontained genetic anomaly, one of the so-called Tinkers, is responsible for the recent devastation on Circula Fardawn Station."

On the screen, an image appears of a gray oblong hanging against a starry sky. Two curving arms sweep out from the main body, like the arms of a twirling dancer.

Suddenly one of the arms brightens, flaring red, then blinding white. It explodes, sending a shower of glittering debris across the sky.

Nola gasps. Theon swears. Everyone in the cafeteria is riveted to the devastation on that screen.

The reporter goes on. "The official death count stands at 253, but is expected to rise. Dunosse Frexim, President of the Core Council, had this statement on the tragedy."

The image switches again, now showing a man standing at a podium and speaking vigorously. "I call on all citizens to report any suspected genetic anomalies to their local Governance Authority. We must ensure that these random and dangerous elements are provided the guidance and control they need to be productive members of society."

The woman with the plastic voice comes back on. "Our hearts go out to all those affected by this tragedy. The Red Hands have set up a dedicated netlink for those seeking information about survivors or interested in giving a donation. Thank you, and good night."

The screen winks out. Silence fills the room. Then Syzygy turns her mirrored eyes toward the Clown table and raises one hand to point right at me. She clicks her thumb and says, "Bang!"

I stare back in confusion for a split second. Then my Chocolate Supernova explodes, covering me in sweet, sticky syrup.

"How long do you think it'll be before they stop calling me 'Supernova'?" I groan, tossing myself down on the bed.

Nola, perched cross-legged on her own bed, winces. "People *still* call Jom 'Mooner.' It was right after he came on board and he'd just started fiddling with the autocook. He was trying to make salad dressing, but it came out as some sort of acid. And then he didn't realize and wiped his hands on his pants and, well . . ." Nola blushes, ducking her head slightly.

I can't help giggling. "Okay, I'll take being publicly drenched in chocolate over that any day. I wish I could get the stuff off, though." I sigh, noticing yet another smear of chocolate on my elbow. Three runs through the sonic showers apparently were not enough. "Too bad for Jom, though. He seems nice." I watch Nola carefully.

"Oh, he is!"

"He's *especially* nice to you."

"What? No, he's just . . . really? You think so?"

"Did you not notice the ginormous Chocolate Supernova he gave you?"

"That was an accident. It didn't *mean* anything."

I snort. "If you say so." I lift up the covers and crawl into bed. On the other side of the room, Nola does likewise after hanging her know-it-all carefully from a hook beside her bed. I toss mine onto the floor.

The lights flick out, leaving the room in a starlit darkness.

I stare into the spangled blackness, fidgeting as I try to get comfortable with the lump of the meteorite under my head. I don't dare leave it out. I already almost lost it when Nola got carried away showing me how to use the laundry system. She probably thought I was insane, throwing myself down the chute to grab my chocolate-covered jacket. Maybe I should show it to her. She's nice, and smart, and I don't want to keep secrets from her. But . . .

You have to keep it secret. Can you promise to do that, Beatrix?

I need more information. I wonder if there are any books on it in the library. *The Dummy's Guide to Mysterious Family Heirlooms.* But am I really keeping it secret because of my promise? Or am I scared I might find out I don't really belong here, that my pink hair is all some weird side effect?

"What is it?" Nola asks.

"Huh?"

"You groaned. You aren't still worrying about the Supernova thing, are you?"

"No, I—" But I can't say it, not yet. I curl my fingers around the meteorite, clutching it to my chest. "I was thinking about that news report. Do you really think it was a Tinker-touched person who blew up that space station?"

"Some of us have some pretty, well, terrifying powers. I mean, look at what Sirra can do. If she wanted to, she could cause some serious damage."

"You think someone *wanted* to blow up the station?"

"It could be. Not everyone joins the circus. And not everyone stays."

"Right. Theon told me about the Outcasts. You think they blew up the space station?"

"Maybe," says Nola. "Or it might have been someone who didn't even know they were Tinker-touched, and woke up one day like you did, except instead of pink hair, they . . ."

"Blew up a space station," I finish. "Sounds like it might've been better all around if you guys had found them instead of me."

"No, don't say that, Trix. We don't know. Even Syzygy doesn't know. You're the one we got, and I'm glad you're here. Besides, who knows? You might manifest an even worse power."

"Gee, thanks. No need to sound so cheerful about it. Aren't you worried I might blow you up in the middle of the night?"

"Of course not," says Nola in a falsely serious voice. "I patched an auto-ejector into your bed to spit you out into space if you start going supernova on me."

I giggle, and my grip on the meteorite relaxes. I still can't get over the fact that I've got a friend. I've seen other Bleeker girls laughing like this, teasing and joking with one another, the way you can only pull off when you know you're friends underneath it all. "Hey, Nola. Thanks. For everything."

"S'okay. Good night, Trix."

"Good night."

* * *

The next week is pretty much the best week ever. The new Firedance smokes the old one. Sure, it's going to take twice as much work to get it down, but we're all jazzed about it. I have a table to sit at. I have friends. People still call me Supernova, but I don't care. I love it all. The only downside is the pile of schoolwork Miss Three saddles us with.

I slump down in my chair in the library, letting my head thump back against the smooth metal. About a bazillion pages of tiny print scroll by on the screen in front of me. I flick on my know-it-all and get Britannica to patch me through to Nola. "Remind me again why I'm busting my ass to write an essay on Core Governance Mining Regulations?"

"For your second career as a prospector?" says Nola.

I wince as a shriek of grinding metal bursts out of the

earpiece. "Are you tearing the autosalon apart with your bare hands? Weren't you only giving it a tune-up?"

There's another distant crash. "Yes," she replies, but I'm not sure which question she was actually answering.

"Seriously, though. Give me one good reason I need to know this stuff."

"Because if you don't, Miss Three won't give you your stipend and then you won't be able to come out with me and have fun at the Hasoo-Pashtung Bazaar?"

I sigh. "I can't believe the Ringmaster puts up with this."

"I don't think he puts up with it so much as he runs screaming in terror from the prospect of being responsible for anything so mundane." The clatter in the background sounds like a freight train dancing the tango. "Listen, Trix, I have to go. But I'll help you with the essay tonight if you want."

"Thanks, Nola."

She clicks off. I spend about a half-hour trying to make sense of a single subclause about the use of sonic liquifiers before I start to feel like someone used a sonic liquifier on my brain. Leaving the study carrel, I decide to check the shelves again for anything that might give me a clue about my meteorite.

Last time it took me an hour to get through a single shelf. Nothing is in any sort of order. I guess I could check out the catalogue window thing, but honestly, it's kind of fun looking through this stuff. Some of it I recognize: the collected works of Shakespeare, a bunch of shonen manga, and the Time-Life "Supernatural" series. Most of it, though, is stuff like *Pipelines: Miracle or Menace?* and *101 Recipes for Paccadi Nuts* and *A Brief History of the Centaurus Corporation* (which is, I kid you not, a foot thick).

A muffled thump turns me toward the door, wondering if I've got company. I don't see anyone. The next moment I yelp as Miss Three materializes right in front of me. She smirks at the book in my hands. *Love Among the Stars: The True Story.*

"Hard at work on your essay, I see." Her eyes track the room like laser beams, then return to my face. "Where is he?"

"Who?"

"The Ringmaster. He knows how important it is that we review the accounting records in a timely fashion, and yet he insists on running off, when we're already five performances behind, and—what is it, Miss Ling?"

I could swear I saw a flash of sequins around the edge of the doorway, but I latch my gaze back onto Miss Three.

"Nothing. There's no one else here. Just me, doing my essay."

She frowns. A spider web of static crosses her ghostly face as she spins, slowly, toward the door.

"Hey, have you checked the autosalon? Nola's working on it. Maybe he's over there. Supervising."

It's a lame excuse, but she halts, studying me.

"You should check over there," I say.

I almost smell the ozone crackling off her response. "I know his ways, Miss Ling. He can't hide forever." Then she winks out.

"You can come out now," I say. "She's gone."

The Ringmaster steps out from the entryway gingerly, his eyes darting around the room. Then he pulls the top hat from his head, brushes back his mane of dark hair, and heaves an enormous sigh. "Thank you, Beatrix, for saving me from a fate that requires only the barest smidge of hyperbole to merit the term 'worse than death.'"

"No problem," I say. "Not that I'm a fan of crunching the numbers, either, but how long do you think you can play hide-and-seek?"

"Oh, I suppose I'll have to deal with it eventually," he says, leaning against the wall. He quirks one brow at me. "Rather like your essay, I imagine."

"Don't remind me."

He twiddles his hat in his hand for a moment, giving me a speculative look. "Would you care for a break? A little excitement and mystery and quite probably danger?"

I toss my book aside. "As long as it doesn't involve the twelve subclauses on the Shovel Hygiene Ordinance, I'm good to go."

CHAPTER 10

The Lighthouse

W HOA." MY BREATH FOGS the viewport glass as I press myself against it, staring at the needle of gold hanging in the black void beyond. "What did you say it's called?"

"The Lighthouse," says the Ringmaster. He's more jittery than I am, spinning his baton from hand to hand like it might burn him if he holds it too long.

"And why did the Tinkers build it?"

"This particular lighthouse once helped to guide ships through the Anvaran dust clouds. But all the lighthouses served as strongholds for the Tinkers. They were places of learning and teaching: way stations from which to reach out across the universe."

"Then there's more of them?" I squint. The Lighthouse is a lot closer now. It's hard to judge size, but it looks big. Like, city-skyscraper big.

"So the legends say. This is the only one I've found." The Ringmaster stares fixedly out the viewport, as if the whole entire ginormous Lighthouse might vanish if he looked away for even a millisecond.

"I don't get it, though. If it's a Tinker clubhouse, why is it so dangerous?" Outside, the boarding tube snakes out from the Big Top to link us to the Lighthouse.

"If the light itself were to activate while we were on board, it would be rather like sunbathing on Venus."

I cross my arms. "So will it hurt the Big Top if it lights up?"

"No, the Big Top has solar shielding. Out there we'll be unprotected. But it's probably completely inactive now." He gives an airy wave.

"Probably? So, what, we have only a five percent chance of getting burned to a crisp?"

"It wouldn't be fun without a little danger, now, would it?" The Ringmaster's smile is like the noonday sun, so bright you're sure nothing terrible could ever happen as long as it's blazing down on you. "Besides, you can hardly expect to find anything interesting somewhere safe."

A shiver runs through the floor as the far end of the boarding tube clamps onto the golden needle. The doorway to the tube hisses open, waiting for us. The Ringmaster holds out a hand. I take it, and together we race along the passage to the airlock that will take us onto the Lighthouse.

The Ringmaster hands me a breathing mask. "Just in case," he says lightly. He's got another stuffed into one of his sequined coat pockets. "Think of it, Beatrix. We're about to walk in the footsteps of the ancients. Are you ready?" He rests a hand lightly on the sealed tunnel before us. He's grinning like a madman. And maybe he is mad, and I guess I am, too, because I can feel the enormous goofy smile plastered on my own face. But come on, we're about to explore an ancient alien space station. I think a little madness is understandable.

As the door hisses open, the Ringmaster pulls out what looks like an old-fashioned gold pocket watch. He flips it open briefly, then slides it back into his coat. He glances back, toward the Big Top, and for a moment he looks almost . . . guilty.

"I really don't think an hour is going to make a difference," I say.

"What?"

"Miss Three. You know, the number crunching. You looked worried. But this is more important, right?" I frown. "Is the translator not getting this?"

"Miss Three, of course. Yes," he says, talking rapidly, as if trying to escape the conversation. "Right, let's go."

Man. The Ringmaster isn't the easiest book to read, but today I feel like he's written upside down, backwards, and in Swahili. I shrug it off and follow him into the Lighthouse.

We move slowly at first, as the Ringmaster lingers over every niche, every scrap of metal, even the light fixtures. "Hah, still on standby! And the artificial gravity is working," he says, fiddling with a panel in the wall. A murky amber glow fills the corridor. "Good old Tinker technology. And they say we're not reliable." The light begins to sputter. The Ringmaster gives the panel a thump, and the flickering stops.

"And look at this!" He darts forward to jam nearly his entire upper body into a shadowy recess. His voice echoes from the wall. "The recycling system! Imagine it, Beatrix! The first Tinker might have once stood here, tossing away a candy wrapper."

I cross my arms, leaning against the wall while he extracts his head. "So you brought me to see the ancient alien garbage disposal. You sure know how to show a girl a good time."

He gives me an injured look. "Recycling systems can be quite fascinating, I assure you. You should visit the one on the Big Top. It's an experience you won't forget."

"Sorry," I say, hastening to catch up as he takes off

again down the corridor. "I guess I was expecting something a little more . . . whoa."

"Like this?" The Ringmaster leads the way out into a massive open space. Bigger than the Big Top tent. So big I can't see the far side. A narrow walkway edged by softly gleaming lights stretches out into the void. The Ringmaster lifts his baton, the gem on the top flaring to life.

Suddenly a thousand lights are winking back at us, reflected in the glossy walls that swoop up into unseen heights and down into the abyss. I can make out the distant sparkle of the far side now.

The entire center of the Lighthouse is hollow. "What is this place?" My voice comes out as a whisper. It's like being in a church, somehow. The age, I guess, and the silence. The feeling that I'm standing on top of generations of pain and joy and striving.

"This is the lantern chamber, the source of the light itself. When the Lighthouse is active, this chamber reflects and concentrates the beacon. And consequently would burn us to a crisp."

"And that?" I point to the slice of darkness hanging in the center of the chamber, tethered by the narrow walkway.

The Ringmaster grins. "That is the heart of the entire station. The Keeper's Watch. If there's anything interesting here, that's where we're going to find it."

We cross the walkway in the golden circle cast by

the Ringmaster's baton. I glance over the edge. It's enough to lodge a bowling ball in my throat. Anybody who falls here is going to have a long, long time to regret it.

When we're about halfway across, I think I see something. A flicker in the reflected lights, like something's moving in front of them. Then nothing. I shake myself sharply. Come on, Trix. Next you'll be saying you saw the Mizzebar Moon Monster.

Still, I can't help but sigh a little in relief when we duck into the black dome of the Keeper's station, away from the abyss and the chilly gusts that flow up like the breath of some nasty monster waiting below.

We find out soon enough that the monster has already been and gone and left his calling card. Panels hang open, revealing banks of blackened wire. Screens sit dead and dark, drifts of shattered glass littering the floor around them. The room is totaled.

With a savage curse, the Ringmaster kicks aside a pile of broken metal, sending it rocketing out of the room. The violent clatter turns to utter silence as the debris tumbles off the edge of the walkway and into the void. It makes my skin crawl.

"What do you think happened?" I ask.

The Ringmaster whips around, teeth bared, baton raised as if to smash the long-gone vandals. It's more than a little terrifying. "The Mandate. They destroyed it, as they destroy everything!"

"Hey!" I catch hold of his arm before he can bash anything else. He starts to shake me off, but I hang on. "I like to hit things when I get angry, too, but can't we use any of this stuff?"

The fury washes out of his face like I socked him with a bucket of cold water. He drops his arm, digging the end of the baton into the floor and leaning heavily against it. "I thought—hoped—there might be . . ." He coughs, and I can't make out the last word. It might have been "answers."

The Ringmaster raises a hand to his throat, his breath rasping. Slumping against the wall, he pulls the breathing mask from his pocket and presses it to his mouth. Closing his eyes, he draws a long, rattling breath. He takes three more hits, then lowers the mouthpiece and rests his head back against the wall. I've never seen him look so young, or so . . . fragile. It scares me enough that I scramble for a joke.

"You okay?" I ask. "Or do you need a time-out?"

He winces, then chuckles. "I suppose I deserved that. No, no more tantrums. Only . . . regret."

"Are you sure there's nothing here?" I search the floor around us for anything that isn't blackened, smashed, or shattered. I spot a few bits of crystal that look like the datastores Nola gave me to download onto from the universal net. "What about those?"

His lips twist as he scoops up a handful. "Broken. I

suppose Miss Three might be able to recover something, but the chances are—"

I stiffen upright. "Did you hear that?" A slithering noise whispers against my ears. "There!"

The Ringmaster pushes himself away from the wall, searching the darkness. His eyes widen, looking past me.

I follow his gaze in time to see something bleed through the darkness, a darting crimson needle. The Ringmaster pulls me closer, to the center of the circle of light that falls from his baton. "Stay in the light, Beatrix."

"What are they?"

"Imagine every quality that would be desirable in a living weapon, culled by the Mandate from a universe of deadly genetic potential. Put them all together, and you have the Vycora. They are fast, they are implacable, and they can slice us through before we even feel the pain of it. They have only one weakness. Light."

"So we're safe here?" I spin around, searching the edge of the pool of golden light.

"For now. But I can't—" Another fit of coughing doubles him over. As the baton dips, our frail circle of protection shifts. I step sideways, grabbing the Ringmaster's arm to keep him upright. Something slithers over my foot. I kick it away, terror digging sharply into my spine. But it's only a coil of blackened wires.

The Ringmaster raises the mask to his face again. For a long moment the only sounds are his strained breathing and the skin-crawling slither of the Vycora. Then he puts the mask aside and looks at me intently.

"Beatrix, do you trust me?"

It feels, somehow, as if this is the most important question anyone has ever asked me. "Yes."

He gives me a brief, dazzling smile before scrambling upright and heading for the nearest of the smashed consoles. He begins ripping through them, pulling out the innards.

"Um. But I'd still like to know what you're doing."

"Turning on the Light. Aha!" He brandishes a handful of colorful wires, then begins twisting them together, like he's hot-wiring a car. "It should drive off the Vycora."

"I thought you said the Light would fry us."

"Only if we don't get back to the Big Top before it reaches full power."

"Which will take how long?"

"Twenty-three seconds. Plus or minus."

"Getting burned to a crisp is a definite minus." I bounce on my heels. All I can think of is the time I spilled hot grease on my hand as a little girl, helping my mom fry spring rolls. And how much it hurt. But crazy as it sounds, I do trust the Ringmaster. "Starting when?"

"Now." He dances back from the console as a hum pulses through the floor. Light begins to pour out from somewhere above us: a pure, white brilliance that makes me blink.

We run, racing between the killing darkness and the blinding light. My mind is empty of everything but the pounding of my feet and the dark outline of the distant door. Scarlet threads slide across our path, but the claws of brilliance tear them away.

A moment later the light begins to tear at us, too. I hear the Ringmaster hiss. Spines of white-hot fire jab into my skin. Tears stream down my cheeks, burned out of my eyes.

The light chases us all the way back to the Big Top. Even as the airlock hisses closed, I can see bright beams reaching out from the Lighthouse. It's like a star being born. The terror and the wonder of it nearly knocks me to the floor. Relief turns my knees to jelly, but at the same time there's an ache deep inside. It's like someone handed me a book of secrets and only let me see one page before snatching it back again.

I punch the control panel beside the windows, darkening the glass. The light streaming through the viewport dies to a distant glow. The Ringmaster leans against the wall, resting his head against the gently humming metal and drawing a long breath. "I'm sorry."

For a moment, I'm not entirely sure he's talking to me. "Are you hurt?" he asks.

"No. You?"

He shakes his head. "We achieved a dazzlingly successful escape, if nothing else." He sighs, extracting a handful of broken crystal from his pocket. It's the crushed datastore.

"What did you expect to find?" I say at last.

The Ringmaster smiles faintly. "Oh, the usual things. Answers to the eternal questions. The meaning of life." He turns the bits of crystal in his hand. "The trouble with being the leader is that people tend to expect you to be leading them somewhere in particular." He looks up then, and for once his eyes don't hold galaxies, only uncertainty and pain. He's never looked more human.

I feel like somebody's offered me a key, for this brief, fragile moment, to unlock a part of the mystery that is the Ringmaster. I don't know how long it will last, and there's so much I want to ask. When I open my mouth, the question that comes out surprises even me.

"Are you happy being the Ringmaster?"

He closes his eyes and rests his palms against the wall. The Big Top hums. His lips tighten.

"It wasn't supposed to be a stumper," I say finally.

The Ringmaster's eyes stay closed. "Life is about choices, Beatrix. But when you choose one road, it means there are others you may never walk. Things you sacrifice . . ."

"What kind of things?"

He looks at me then. "It's more than a title, being the Ringmaster. The Big Top is my responsibility. She is mine and I am hers. Which means I can't be . . ." He stops himself, giving a sort of half-shrug. "But it was my choice. I've seen things, done things, been things I could never have otherwise. And I would never give it up. *Ever.*" The Big Top thrums again, more loudly. His lips twist. "Though perhaps she deserves better."

"No," I say. "I'm just the new girl and all, but from what I've seen, I think the Big Top is lucky to have you. We all are."

The Ringmaster cocks his head, speaking to the walls. "You hear that? I take her out and nearly get her burned to a crisp and she says I'm doing a good job." He sighs, glancing down to the crushed datastore bits. "And I thought I might find answers. It was foolhardy, but I'm a fool if nothing else."

The meteorite weighs in my pocket as if it's trying to compact into a black hole. I hear Dad's warning, as clear as ever. *You have to keep it secret. You have to protect it.* But the Ringmaster has given me his secrets, or at least some of them. I want to . . . honor that. To share a secret of my own. I can't find the right words, so in the end I just stick out my hand, the black oblong smooth in my palm.

There's a flicker of something in his face, too quick for me to catch. He brushes the tip of one finger over the meteorite, tracing the thin crack.

I force myself to speak. "My parents gave it to me. I thought maybe . . . maybe it's important. They made me promise to keep it safe, and Nyl sure wanted to get his hands on it, so I figure it must be the real deal."

He's still staring.

"Or maybe it's a pretty rock," I add.

"No. The Tinkers made this. But made it for what?" He takes it, holding it aloft and frowning.

"And why did my parents have it?" I search his face for answers. "They must have been Tinker-touched, too." My hands are shaking. "Right? That must be it. Why else would they have it?"

"Indeed." The Ringmaster gives me an inscrutable look, then presses the meteorite back into my hand. "Thank you. For trusting me enough to show me this." He hesitates, then adds, "It might be wise to allow Miss Three to study it."

"No! I mean, why? If it's a Tinker antique, what would she know? Besides, she's from the Mandate. I don't—"

"Trust her?"

I fiddle with the meteorite, tumbling it between my fingers. "Not yet. But I've got someone else I want to show it to."

* * *

"It looks like a rock to me," says Nola. She turns the meteorite to catch the brightest beams from the lamp, then shakes her head. "If the Ringmaster didn't know, I'm not sure I can do any better."

"The Ringmaster isn't a Tech genius," I say, bouncing on the edge of my bed.

"I guess I could run some tests," Nola offers. She roots around inside one of the flip-out drawers beside her bed, pulling out a selection of tools. "There must be something inside, if it heated up. But you said that was the first time?"

"Yeah. I wonder why? Maybe it was reacting to my Tinker-touch. It happened that same night my hair turned pink. The same night Nyl found me." I suppress a shiver at the memory, and try not to think about where he might be now.

Nola shrugs. "Could be that. Could be chance. Could be something else completely." Nola slides one of her tools over the surface of the rock, frowning. "Has it always had the crack?"

"No." I fill her in on my first encounter with Nyl. "So if bashing him in the face with the meteorite didn't bust it, dropping it onto the floor must have."

"Hmmm. It's not actually a meteorite. It's artificial. A pretty durable composite." By this time Nola has gone through a half-dozen scanners, gauges, and something that looks like an eggbeater, but the furrow between her brows has only gotten deeper. "I'm surprised it cracked at all. Hey, what's this?"

"You found something?"

"Maybe." Nola squints at the display on her egg-beater. "I'm picking up some microwave radiation."

"So . . . I can use it to make a bag of popcorn?"

Nola frowns, twiddling a dial. "It could be a signal, or a message. Or a beacon." She lifts her eyes. "But I know one thing it definitely is not."

"What?"

"An essay on Core Governance Mining Regulations."

I groan, flopping back onto the bed. "It's going to be a long night."

CHAPTER 11

Secrets in the Dark

'M ON FIRE. Struggling out of sleep, I find myself twisted in my sheets, slick with sweat. Even through my pillow I can feel the warmth pulsing from the rock. I throw back the covers, feeling disgustingly damp.

I fumble for the rock. It's warm, but not too hot to handle. Across the room Nola mumbles something in her sleep. We were both up late: me because Core Mining Regulations make zero sense, and Nola because she's a saint and helped me with the essay. I'm not keen on making her miss any more sleep because of me, so I slip out into the hall as quietly as I can.

It might be my imagination, but I could swear the rock is getting warmer. I head down the hallway. My fingers flinch from the heat cupped in my hands. It's definitely getting hotter. I head for the bathroom, in case I need to play firefighter.

Except that now the rock is cool again. What kind of game is this? Is it trying to drive me insane?

Or is it trying to send me a message? I back up. Heat stirs against my palm. Gotcha! I take another step, letting the heat lead me along the corridors, out of the dorms, all the way to—

A hallway. A really *boring* hallway. I don't get it. The rock is so hot now I have it bundled in the hem of my shirt. But there's nothing here. I spin around, searching. Then inspiration strikes. I kneel down.

An even stronger wave of heat flows off the rock, pushing me back a step. So maybe it *is* leading me somewhere. I'm just not on the right level. As I stand there, trying to decide how seriously Nola would bust my ass if I started pulling up floor panels from her ship, I realize the rock has gone cool. Wonderful.

I'm about to try to find my way back to my room when I hear a noise. Someone else is moving along the corridor, somewhere beyond the next curve, out of sight. I shrink back against the shadowy arch of the hall. Muffled footsteps pad away. Whoever it was, she's going the other direction.

There's nothing for it. I have to find out what's up.

Rounding a curve in the corridor, I catch a glimpse of someone with long dark hair. Sirra. And I've got a good guess where she's headed.

I keep my distance, trying to walk as quietly as I can. It gets harder as we move into the really cluttered corridors.

Something tickles my toes. Feathers. I spot the remaining hatboxes, still piled against the wall. Somewhere in the distance a burst of static crackles. I stay skulking behind the hatboxes, listening hard. This time I'm going to find out what Sirra is up to.

I can barely make out her silhouette under the dim blue track lights that run along the ceiling. The noises coming out of the wall are still gibberish, but I can hear Sirra well enough.

"No, not yet," she says. "I need more time. I have a plan. Send it to me. But not there. It'll take too long."

More gabble, then Sirra again, sounding annoyed. "Fine, never mind. Make it Hasoo-Pashtung. I'll figure something out."

Hasoo-Pashtung. It's one of the scheduled performance stops, a couple of months down the road, the one Nola keeps talking about because it's got some ginormous shopping bazaar.

There's another sputter from the wall. "I know! I know it's my fault! But no one else will find out. I need to get her alone, and then I can settle everything, I promise. It'll all be over soon." Silence fills the corridor, broken only by a gulping breath.

Something prods me in the shoulder. I bite down on a yelp of surprise as Nola's round face emerges from the shadows. "Trix, what are you doing?" she whispers.

"Better question is, what's Sirra doing?"

"Coming this way! Quick, in here." Nola lays a hand on the wall beside us. The metal scrolls open, revealing a dark recess. We tumble inside.

The walls zip closed, leaving us in near total darkness. A small slitted window lets in a slice of the dim blue light from outside. We watch in silence as Sirra marches past our hiding spot.

"What is this?" I ask, after I'm sure Sirra is gone.

"Storage closet. Though obviously *some* people have a different notion of what that means. Did you see all that clutter out there? And here's this perfectly good closet, not a foot away, empty!" Nola taps the wall. It folds open obligingly.

"Lucky for us," I say, following her out. "I don't think Sirra would have been happy to find someone eavesdropping, even if we only heard half the conversation. Why wasn't the translator handling the other voice?"

Nola frowns. "Some sort of scrambler, maybe. Come on, I'll take a look."

I pace back and forth, scuffing up clouds of feathers, while Nola studies the communication panel. "Yeah, someone definitely didn't want anyone listening in on that call."

"Can you tell where it came from? Who it was?"

Nola shakes her head. "Someone off-ship. What was she saying? I only heard the last part."

I fill her in, describing the most recent conversation as well as the one I stumbled into when I first came on board.

"I wonder who she needs to get alone?"

"And why." I frown. "She's up to something."

"Do you think we should tell the Ringmaster?"

"No," I say quickly, remembering his attitude at brunch. "First we get proof."

"That's about all I can do right now. I guess we should get back to the dorm. If we can even find the way." Nola grimaces. "I was in such a rush to follow you, I forgot to grab my know-it-all."

I point down the corridor. "It shouldn't be too hard to go back the way we—"

An eerie wailing cuts off my words. A moment later, the corridor I was pointing at is gone, replaced by a blank gray wall.

The hallway lights turn orange. Nola yelps. "The ship's compacting! We've got to get out of here!"

Only one choice. We race down the remaining corridor. Metal crunches and slams behind us. I keep my eyes ahead, willing the walls to stay put just a little longer. "What's a safe spot?"

"Our beds get capsuled, but they're probably cut off already."

"Where else?"

"The bridge, the library, the commons, the bio-habitat."

"Great. Where are they?" We've reached a junction. Two orange-lit corridors twist away, right and left.

"I—I don't know. I don't know where we are, Trix. I don't have my know-it-all. We're going to get smashed!" Nola's voice spirals up into a squeak of fear.

"No, we're not!" I scan the walls, looking for anything familiar. "What about another closet?"

"If I knew where one was. Maybe—eeeee!" Her voice ends in another squeal as the right-hand hallway slams shut.

"It's okay. I know how to get out of here! This way!" Seizing Nola's hand, I pull her with me down the remaining corridor. "I was in this hall the other night. I remember that light was out, see there? A little farther there's a turn . . . aha! And then there was a door that goes into—"

We burst out into an open green space. One last crash of compacting metal echoes behind us. Both of us go sprawling across the grass of the biohabitat. I have just enough time to enjoy my three-dimensional state before everything melts to the familiar blackness of the jump.

* * *

"See? It's better than last time, isn't it?" says Nola.

"Oh, sure." I rub my gummy eyes. "This time I only feel like I've been dipped in glue and hung upside down for a few hours. Much better." I stand up shakily.

The Ringmaster's voice echoes from the walls.

"Attention, Galacticus Crew! As you may have noted, we took a bit of a detour. I'm afraid the Big Top took it upon herself to jump us into the Jerrindar System."

Nola gives a low whistle. "That's not good."

"While it's my hope this is merely the result of the Big Top conceiving an urgent and inescapable craving for Jerrindarian Toffee, you may be assured that Miss Three and I will be investigating fully. In the meantime we ask you all to remain in your dorms. Please, go back to sleep; you'll need your strength in the morning. We've acquired some leeches, and you know what that means."

Nola groans.

"Leeches?" I ask. "Like the nasty little things that suck your blood?"

Nola makes a face. "No, like the nasty *big* things that suck on the Big Top's energy field. They're disgusting." She shivers. "But leeches bother me a lot less than the Big Top jumping on her own."

"Do you think Sirra had something to do with it?"

Nola taps a finger against her chin. "It's possible. If the Big Top detected a gravity well, it might set off the proximity warnings for a black hole, and that would cause a jump. But why would she do it, Trix?"

"I don't know," I admit. "Still, it's pretty suspicious that she was the only one prowling around when it happened."

"Actually, she wasn't the only one." Nola gives me a meaningful look.

"Oh. Right. But we didn't do anything."

Nola doesn't look entirely convinced. "I'm not sure Miss Three would see it that way."

"No, as a matter of fact. She does not."

"Uh-oh," says Nola.

Yeah, we're toast. Miss Three flickers into view, a severe, dark ghost floating above the greenery. "Would you two please explain what you are doing out of your dorms in the middle of the night?"

"Ahh . . ." Nola opens her mouth and flaps her hands, looking like a fish out of water.

"It was my fault," I say. "I was sleepwalking. Nola came after me to wake me up, but then the alarm went off, so we had to come here to not get squashed. Sorry," I add, aware that I don't sound particularly apologetic.

"And I suppose you had nothing to do with that unplanned jump?"

"No," says Nola, her nervousness bubbling over. "How could we? Even I don't know how to make the Big Top jump. I've tried to see what the Ringmaster does, but it's something with that baton of his, and I can't quite make it out, so you see we couldn't—"

"Enough, Miss Ogala. I assure you we will be getting

to the bottom of this matter soon enough. For the time being, kindly return to where you are supposed to be, and stay there. We will see about suitable recompense for curfew violations tomorrow."

Thankfully the decompaction bell sounds. Nola and I beat a hasty retreat back to our dorm.

CHAPTER 12

Leeches

I T'S A PUNISHMENT, that's what it is," says Nola glumly. "If this was a random chore assignment, I'm the Wazeer of Deneb."

"Is it really that bad?" I grit my teeth as I shove my foot into one of the tall white spaceboots. I'm already wearing the suit; it's hard to believe something so crinkly-thin is going to keep me safe in the big black void.

"Is it that bad? Hah!" says Theon as she buckles on her own boots. "Ask your know-it-all to find you some pictures of Anvaran dust cloud leeches. No, wait; ask for pictures of the sucker scars, so you see what you're really getting into."

Besides the three of us, there are five others on leech-removal duty: Sirra, Etander, Ghost, a Tech boy named Toothy, and the walking boulder I've seen at the Freak table. He introduces himself as Gravalon Pree in a voice as rich and rumbly as Rocky Road ice cream. He's the only one besides me who seems excited about the mission.

"But we get to fly around with those spacewings," I say. "That's got to be amazing!"

Nola shudders. "That's the worst part."

"But it sounds like fun. Isn't it?"

"Maybe for you. I get sick."

"You should stay midship, Nola," says Sirra. "Trix can handle the aft section on her own. She's always up for a challenge."

Right, like Sirra's suddenly some kind of guardian angel. It has nothing to do with getting me alone out on the hull. Nola looks at me, clearly thinking the same thing. "No, I'm Trix's partner. I'll stay with her."

Sirra shrugs. Clicking down the seal on her helmet, she heads for the airlock, where the others are waiting. She doesn't have any spacewings. I guess with her fancy gravity-bending superpowers, she doesn't need solar-powered jets. Gravalon Pree, on the other hand, doesn't seem to need a spacesuit, but with his extra-large space-wings he looks like some sort of overgrown rock fairy.

While Nola is off checking something on the airlock,

I pull on my own wings. They slip on over my shoulders, but I can't lower my arms. I crane my neck, but I can't see what's wrong. Worse, they won't come off. I'm stuck looking like a complete idiot, flailing around with my arms in the air.

I'm about to do something supremely violent to the wings when suddenly they slide down into place. I turn to see who saved me, expecting to see Nola. "Thanks. I was afraid I'd be stuck that way for—"

It's Etander. "—ever."

Immediately my eyes go to his hands. Today they look perfectly normal. I wrench my attention back to his face. "Oh. Hey. Thanks."

"They were caught up in back," he says quietly.

"Um . . ." Should I ask how he's doing? Or would that only make things more awkward?

He saves me from my social disorder by going on. "About what happened last week . . . we shouldn't have tried to kick you out of the Ring. I'm sorry about . . . about everything that happened."

"Hey, no problem. We're good," I say. "I mean, if you're all—"

"Are you looking forward to testing out the space-wings?" he interrupts, eyes darting away from my unfinished question.

Okay. I guess we're done with that topic. "Sure," I say. "Sounds like fun. And a little dangerous."

"You don't seem afraid."

"Hey, as long as I don't end up covered in chocolate with a new nickname, I think I'll be happy."

That wins me a smile. "Good luck, then."

Theon calls for everyone's attention. "All right, people, time for a safety-procedure chat. I know everyone else has heard it before, but we've got Trix with us for the first time, and you all can use a reminder, so listen up."

"Yes, Miss Three," says the Tech boy in an undertone. Theon scowls at him.

"In case you've forgotten, Toothy, we almost had Dragon doing a space dive into the nearest star last time we went out on spacewings. This is seriously dangerous."

I can feel Etander's eyes on me, and I ignore them.

"Now, there are three rules to remember: First, don't get too far from the ship. This isn't the time for joyriding. Second, don't use your blasters"—she pats the blunt black rod hanging from her belt—"until you pry the leech free. We don't want to accidentally breach the hull.

"And third, if someone gets suckered by a leech, remember to use your beacon." She taps the palm-size disk hanging beside her blaster. "Press the button and give it a good throw, as far away from yourself and the Big Top as possible."

"What does it do?" I ask.

"Lets off an energy signal that attracts the leeches," says Toothy, his grin showing a large number of his namesakes. "I designed it."

"So why can't we trigger a bunch of them to get all the leeches off?"

Toothy's grin fades.

"They have a few side effects," says Nola. "We're working on it."

"What kind of side effects?"

"Well, the worst part is that the energy burst upsets the Big Top's jump system," says Nola. "So we wouldn't be able to jump for at least six hours. It also gives everyone hiccups. We're really not sure why that is."

"So only use it in a real emergency. Everybody got all that?" Theon crosses her arms, looking more than a little like Miss Three. "Good; let's go blast some leeches."

A hiss of decompressing air raises goose bumps along my arms. This is it. In a moment, I'm going to be in space. No glass, no screen; only a thin layer of some wacky alien super-fabric between me and the universe. Okay, so I'll be spending the morning pulling giant leeches off the hull. But I'll be in space! I'm going to fly!

I start to bob as the pull of the ship's artificial gravity ebbs away. Theon and Ghost fly out into the void, followed by Sirra, Etander, and Toothy. With the underwater grace of a humpback, Gravalon Pree dives smoothly through the door, executing an elaborate curvette as he heads off along one finlike ridge of the ship's hull.

Nola pauses, clinging one-handed to the exit, to look back at me. She's saying something. I rap at my helmet.

"Hey, Britannica! I turned you on for a reason. Come on, give me a link to everyone else."

"I beg your pardon," comes the voice of my know-it-all. "I thought you said to be quiet. I was trying to oblige."

"Nola, I want to hear. You, I want quiet. I'm going to hear too much about that stupid show as it is." I stifle a groan. I have *got* to figure out a way to deal with that thing. It took some serious bribery to get it to do what I wanted this morning.

"And you won't regret it!" shrills my know-it-all. "We are going to have *such* a good time watching the marathon! But have a care with those leeches, dear. You've enough of a challenge with that hair. You certainly don't need a sucker scar to worry about."

"Okay, okay, I'll be careful. Now, patch me through."

"—you going to be okay?" Nola's voice comes through so loudly it's like she's right inside my helmet.

"Piece of cake!" I give her a thumbs-up in case the translator doesn't know how to handle that. It's true. I really feel good about this. For as long as I can remember, my sleep has been full of flying dreams. I've probably spent half my nights swooping over trees and into the clouds. I figure it might even have been part of my Tinker-touch. Maybe all those dreams were preparing me for this.

I pat the slight bulge along my side where the rock lies tucked in the pocket of my shirt, under the tinfoil spacesuit. It's not only the rock that got me here. I *am* special. This is what my parents were trained for. This was what I was born for. Space.

Gripping the handholds of my spacewings, I give the thrusters a trial burst. For one glorious moment I'm perfect, an eagle, a comet in the night. Then one wing dips. My hands clench instinctively. Suddenly I'm rocketing forward, careening past Nola and out into space.

It's like flying twelve kites at once in a hurricane. I swing my arms around, trying desperately to stop myself. All I accomplish is turning my flight into an end-over-end tumble. I feel like I left my stomach back on the ship.

Finally I steady myself and come around into a shaky glide. Nola flies over to join me. "Are you okay?" She looks a little green herself, but at least she's staying right-side up.

"Yeah. Just getting a feel for these things." I give the thrusters a gentle tap, enough to keep up with Nola.

"You're doing great. Much better than my first time. Come on, our section is this way."

I grit my teeth, struggling to stay with Nola as she heads off along the rippling red striped hull of the Big Top. So much for my fabulous inborn talent for flying. I'm barely holding my course steady, and it's not like Nola's a speed demon.

But by the time we reach the tail section, I'm a little more confident. I swoop along the ridges and up into the emptiness beyond, trying to get a glimpse of the entire massive ship. Now that I can see it, the Big Top reminds me of some weird undersea creature, like a jellyfish or maybe a pudgy squid. With red stripes.

"Trix, don't go too far!" Nola's voice echoes in my ear. "Remember what Theon said. Anyway, I found some leeches. We'd better get to work."

Reluctantly, I fly back. Nola has already clamped her magnetized boots onto the hull and is hard at work pulling on something that looks like a giant purplish-gray slug. The thing narrows, stretching like a piece of taffy.

It pops free. "Take that!" Nola says, directing her blaster at the leech. It twitches in a halo of crackling blue light, then drifts off into space. She turns to me as I land. "Did you see how I did it? You have to be careful when they let go; that's when they're liable to attack. Want to try one yourself?" She gestures to the hull on either side. About a dozen more leeches have clamped onto the Big Top. The smallest is as long as my forearm. The largest is almost as big as I am.

As we work, Nola chatters away, telling me stories about life on the Big Top. Considering I'm prying giant leeches off a spaceship, I'm having a great time. It's funny; when the Ringmaster offered me this shot at joining the circus, I thought the best thing would be space itself. And it *is* pretty freaking spectacular. Right now I can look up at that dome of stars and know—not just hope—that they're full of life. It's a feeling I can't even put into words. Mom and Dad would have understood it.

But you know what else is just as freaking spectacular? Nola. Here she is, telling me her stories, inviting me into her life like I'm her sister or something, not a random pink-haired tagalong from a boondock galaxy. I'm not all that used to people being nice to me. Pretty much everything that's made me happy since I lost my folks has been something I've made or grabbed for myself.

Nola also fills me in on what she's learned about last night's unplanned jump. Turns out it was a gravity anomaly. And guess what? Our new course means we're headed for Hasoo-Pashtung next. Sirra is *definitely* up to something.

"That's the last of these," says Nola, watching the remnants of the largest leech drift away. She heaves a sigh. "I guess we'd better fly over to the other side and check there, too. I hope I make it without getting sick."

Poor Nola. From the look on her face, I don't think she's exaggerating the danger. There must be something I can do to make this easier on her. "How about you stay here?" I say. "I'll go check it out and come back. No sense in you making yourself sick if there's nothing there."

"Are you sure? It's your first time out on spacewings. And what about Sirra?"

"Positive. I'm practically an expert with these things now, and Sirra's at the other end of the ship. Be back in a flash."

"Okay. Thanks, Trix. But keep the link open. Call if you need help."

I wave, then set off over the ridge to the next valley. Finding it leech-free, I move on, winging up away from the hull to get a better view.

I spot a cluster of leeches. There aren't too many, and the biggest is only about two feet long. "Hey, Nola," I say into the link. "I found a few more, but I can handle them. You stay there, and I'll be back when I'm done. Okay? Nola?"

I tap my helmet. "Nola? Can you hear me?" I wait for a long, silent moment. "Hey, Britannica, want to fill me in on what the space pirate Zendalos has been up to?"

Something is definitely wrong. I better head back, before Nola gets worried.

A web of blue light springs up in front of me. I backwing into a somersault, but the blue light is everywhere, caging me in. I pull free my blaster.

"Nola!" I shout into the link. "Something's happening! I need help!"

"Your friend can't hear you." A familiar voice crackles in my ear. I never thought I'd miss that screechy know-it-all, but right now I'd take all the *Love Among the Stars* factoids in the universe over this voice. "I suggest you not attempt to escape the energy cage. You will find the experience both futile and rather painful."

I whirl around. The tip of one spacewing brushes against the interlacing blue light. "Aaaagggh!" I curl against the agony that tears into me. My fingers spasm. The blaster flies free, spinning off beyond the curved wall of my prison.

"As I said."

My hot breath fogs my helmet as I turn, searching for him. There. Nyl floats a few yards beyond my cage. His batlike spacewings blot out the stars.

"What do you want?" I demand.

"To talk."

"Right. You're one of the Mandate, and all you want is a chat? Next you'll be inviting me in for tea and cookies."

"I see he's gotten to you already with his fairy tales." Nyl drifts closer. Starlight gleams on his mask as he tilts his head. "Don't be so quick to assume you know who is the villain and who is the shining hero."

"Call me crazy, but I'm going to say the villain is the guy who keeps attacking me."

"I am trying to help you. You are on a dangerous path, and if you don't turn back now, you will be lost forever. It may even be too late."

"Thanks for the oh-so-helpful warning, but I'm right where I want to be."

"This isn't a joke! I know the lies the Ringmaster trades in, but you must not believe them. You don't belong here."

"I do, too! He said it himself! He said I'm—"

"Of course," cuts in Nyl. He sighs. "Listen to me, Beatrix. I understand how bewitching that can be. The idea that you are somehow better than others. That you are shaped for some brilliant future. Others may toil and scrabble in menial occupation and mundane lives, but not you, never you. You are . . . *special.*"

On his lips it sounds like a curse.

"Have you ever considered the pain that proceeds from disparity, from difference? You've seen it on your own planet. The wars fought over the color of one's skin or the choice of one's god. That is what comes of this. Is that what you want?"

"Of course not!" I protest. "But you're twisting it all up! I'm not saying I'm better than anyone. I mean, even if I am, I'm not saying they should . . . aaagh! Look, I'm not a lawyer. I can't make it sound all pretty and convincing, but I know you're wrong. That isn't what the Ringmaster is about."

"You seem to think yourself an expert on the Ringmaster. Do not be so certain you know the truth. How much of his precious ship has he even allowed you to see? You don't belong here."

"Yes I *do!*" My voice rises like a little kid's. "My

parents were Tinker-touched, and so am I. This is where I belong!"

"Is that what he told you?"

"Yes!" I snap, even as a part of my brain sifts through the words cluttering my memory. Had he said it? Or only let me think it?

"He deceives you. He does it to protect you, but he only makes you weak. Come with me now." Nyl drifts closer to my cage and extends one arm. The blue fire pulls back, allowing his gray-gloved fingers to slip past. He holds out his hand. "Abandon this folly. Let us cleanse you of the taint before it destroys you. Let me show you that you need not cover your life in spangles and glitter for it to be something glorious. Something happy. I promise you this, Beatrix. If you stay on this ship, it will break your heart."

"You're wrong." The words tear out of my tight throat. I spin around, searching the remorselessly empty sky. Maybe I can force my way through the web, take the pain, and hope I don't black out before I'm free. "I'm staying here. I belong here." I ignore his outstretched hand.

He is silent for so long, holding that pose, I wonder if maybe I've found a way to freeze time. When he finally does speak, it's like a whip crack on my nerves.

"How unfortunate. We had hoped you would come willingly." He balls his fist and pulls it back out of the blue-fire cage. "But willingly or not, you will come."

The orb of light begins to shift, to float upward, away from the Big Top. Crackles of agony dance along my arms as I try and fail to stay away from the walls. I want to scream, not from pain but from frustration. If only I hadn't dropped the stupid blaster, I might be able to fight back!

Wait. I'm *not* completely defenseless. And we're still close enough to the ship that it might work! I grab the leech beacon from my belt. Punching the button, I throw it as hard as I can, right at Nyl.

He grunts as it catches him in the midsection. The flash of light makes me look away. An odd, fizzy feeling runs along my skin.

"Beatrix, you must—*hic*—" he begins. Then the leeches are on him. He disappears under a writhing mass of gray-purple. The blue web winks out. I spread my spacewings and take off.

As I speed over the next ridge, I catch sight of two other white-clad shapes winging toward me. Static crackles in my ear, followed immediately by Nola's voice. "—happened? Trix, are you—*hic*—okay?"

"Nola? I'm—*hic*—all right. Can you hear me?"

"Thank the First Tinker! When I saw the—*hic*—leech beacon go off and you didn't answer, I thought . . . well, it was—*hic*—horrible, so I'm not even going to say it. Are you—*hic*—sure you're okay?"

"What happened?" asks Theon. "Did you—*hic*—get leeched?"

"No."

"Then why did you set off the—*hic*—leech beacon?"

"There was a Mandate ship. The same—*hic*—one, from Earth. Over there."

Theon takes off over the ridge, holding her blaster ready. I follow.

There's nothing. No ship, no dark-winged Mandate agent. Not even any leeches.

"He's gone!"

"Are you sure he was here?" Theon soars up away from the hull to survey nearby space.

"I didn't—*hic*—imagine it! He was here! He was trying—" I cut myself off. My body feels like I just put it through a round in the Arena at level bazillion. And that's nothing compared to the crazy thoughts battering my brain. I won't believe it. I can't.

"Trying what?" asks Nola.

"It was lies," I say, my voice cracking. "Only—*hic*—lies."

CHAPTER 13

Restricted Area

THEY DON'T HATE YOU," says Nola. We're heading for the common room, several days after the de-leeching incident. "It all worked out okay. It didn't slow us down—very much—and everyone stopped hiccuping yesterday."

A rumble like a distant rockslide echoes along the corridor. "Everyone except Gravalon Pree," amends Nola. "But at least they're not calling you Supernova anymore."

"Right. And Leechbomb is *so* much better," I say.

"You're the only one who isn't acting like I'm insane." Toothy hustles past, glaring at me with sleepy, dark-circled eyes. I can't really blame him. He's Gravalon Pree's roommate. "Or giving me the evil eye."

"If you say you saw a Mandate ship, I believe you. There's a lot of strange stuff going on around here lately."

"Coming through!"

We plaster ourselves against the wall as Jom and Frex come barreling along the hallway, whooping and juggling a pair of fluffy lavender slippers between them as they go.

One of the Principals thunders after them, bellowing, "Give them back, you idiots!" He makes a lunge for Frex, who leaps clear at the last moment: onto the ceiling. He races onward, upside down, and doesn't even skip a beat juggling. The slippers continue sailing back and forth between him and Jom.

A crowd follows after them, shouting encouragement to both sides and uniformly ridiculing the slippers. Catching Nola's eye, I can't help but laugh. "Only lately?"

As the mob rampages away down the hall, Nola lifts a hand to adjust her know-it-all. "The recycling system? Are you sure?" She shudders. "I hope this isn't going to involve a visit to Rjool's lair. No, it's fine, I'll check it out." She straightens her shoulders and sighs.

"Trouble?"

"A Tech's work is never done. You'd better go on without me. This shouldn't take long, but the marathon starts in ten minutes, and you don't want to miss the recap show or you'll be completely lost. I'll catch up with you in the common room." With a hasty wave, Nola sets off back down the hallway, leaving me alone. Or nearly alone.

"Don't you worry about getting lost, dear," chimes my know-it-all. "I've got all fifteen seasons indexed by character name, key plot points, and location. I've also cross-referenced every costume item to the appropriate mercantile dynasty and catalogue, customized to your size and coloring. I think you'd look lovely in this blue number Dalana wears in season eleven, episode five."

I blink as the viewscreen scrolls open in front of my eye, displaying a hideous monstrosity of skintight skirts and hugely puffed sleeves. "Isn't that gorgeous?" burbles my know-it-all. "It's from the scene where Dalana confronts Zendalos at the Governance Ball and discovers the true identity of—"

"Over my dead body." I continue along the corridor.

"Really? I do think it's more suited to a ball than a funeral, but of course it's your choice. I'll update your registered last will and testament as soon as I can contact Core Legal Records Bureau."

"I have a will?"

"Oh, yes. Birth certification, school records, everything. Of course it's all forgery; part of the Ringmaster's false identity protocol, since you're actually a heathen from the Excluded Territories. No, dear, not *that* way!"

"Isn't the common room this way?"

"Heavens, no. You should have gone left at the last intersection. This is a restricted area."

I study the hallway before me. It looks like all the rest: curving, gray-brown, lit by recessed orange lights. The flattened remains of a box labeled FRAGILE lean against one wall, the apparent victim of a compaction. "Why is it restricted? Is it dangerous?"

"That information is restricted."

"Says who?"

"That information is restricted."

"And you call yourself a know-it-all."

"I do know it all," says the device. "I just don't tell it all."

I'm about to return to the unrestricted corridor when Nyl's words whisper from my memory. *How much of his precious ship has he even allowed you to see?*

That's it. I click off the know-it-all and march onward.

* * *

You'd think something called a restricted area would be at least a little bit exciting. You know, maybe some captive alien monsters, or top-secret science experiments, or maybe even the Ringmaster's personal quarters. So far I've found a room full of feathered fans, another chock-full of rusty old gears and springs, and lots and lots of long, monotonous corridors. The only danger here is that I might die of boredom. I'm starting to think I'd be better off watching the six-hour *Love Among the Stars* marathon. One more corridor; that's as far as I'm going. If it's more of the same, I'm done here.

I turn the corner and stop, staring at a hallway that is *definitely* not more of the same. It's more like a tunnel than a corridor. The curved walls glow pink. I can't find the light source. It's like the whole place is . . . alive. Ridges ripple along the walls, reminding me in a nasty way of the pictures of brains from my bio book. Or those things in your lungs that get all crusty and gross in smokers.

Well, I *was* looking for something interesting. Better check it out while I have the chance.

I go about five steps before I realize my pocket is giving off heat. I pull out the rock. It's definitely warm to the touch. Hmm.

I take a step back. Like magic, the rock cools down. A step forward, and it's warm again. I hold the infuriating thing up in front of my nose. "So you want to play hot and cold again? Fine. I'm game."

The cerebral tunnel takes me past two arched doorways. By the time I reach the third, the rock is so hot I need to bundle it in a corner of my jacket. As I move on, the heat dies away.

I spin around, facing the third doorway. There's some kind of panel above it. I can't read the funky alien script. I try tapping at the door. All that happens is that the squiggles above it reconfigure into numbers: 1349. Great. That's a lot of help.

There's no lever or knob or anything. "Come on," I tell the door. "I followed the bread crumbs and everything. Let me in!"

The door ignores me. I'm about ready to give it a good kick when I hear voices echoing from back down the corridor behind me. There's only one person on the ship with an electronic buzz to her voice: Miss Three. And I am *not* getting lectured again. I've got no choice but to keep going and hope there's a way out farther down the tunnel.

It sounds like a good plan, except that when I skitter around the next curve, there is no more tunnel. The brainlike walls widen out to encircle a dimly lit open space. It's a dead end.

"It's too great a risk, Ringmaster," says Miss Three behind me. My heart thumps even faster. Bad enough to be caught sneaking around a restricted section by Miss Three. But how can I explain this to the Ringmaster? I've got to hide. But where?

I check out the corrugated walls. The ridges are deeper here, twisting in patterns that almost make sense if you tilt your head and squint. It's my only choice.

Jamming my fingers into one of the grooves, I pull myself up and scramble into the deepest crevice I can find. Ewww. Spaceship walls are not supposed to be damp. Or warm. Or *spongy*. Gah.

I hold my breath as two figures walk into the room below.

"She hasn't caused any serious trouble so far," the Ringmaster is saying.

"The jump systems were offline for nearly eight hours. If we'd been attacked—"

"But we weren't. And if there was a Mandate agent in the area, she can hardly be blamed for panicking."

Hmmph. I did *not* panic. I used the resources I had on hand. That's being clever, not panicking.

"The Big Top sensors reported no such presence," says Miss Three.

"Sensors can be deceived."

"Then I suppose you'll say it was a coincidence I discovered her sneaking around the very same night the Big Top made that unprecedented jump? And how do you propose to explain the strange communications we've been tracking? Someone on this ship is sending illicit messages. Miss Ling is a threat to everything you've built here. The ship itself has not recognized her. I've seen the *Programme*. She's no Principal, whatever you may have hoped. You can't allow her to stay. You know what she *really* is. Why won't you tell her the truth?"

"Only Beatrix knows what she really is, and what she's capable of. I intend to give her the chance to discover that. And whatever the case, she deserves a place on the Big Top as much as I do," says the Ringmaster, a harsher note entering his voice. "Though perhaps that's not the best of arguments." The echoes of his laugh grate against my skin.

"This is hardly the time for laughter."

"Indeed it is! Danger and destruction are everywhere; enemies confront us at every turn; all that we've worked for might come to nothing. It's exactly the right time for a bit of humor. Keeps one sane, you see."

"With such a model of sanity before me, how could I not?"

This time the Ringmaster's laugh holds no sharp edges. "A joke! Very good, Miss Three! You see, you're learning something from me."

"And you would do well to learn from me, Ringmaster. It's why I am here, is it not? That girl is a danger you cannot ignore. She could jeopardize everything."

"Believe me, Miss Three, I'm aware of the danger. But also of the potential. If the former outweighs the latter, I'll know how to act."

"And you are prepared to take extreme measures?"

"Yes."

What? What does that mean?

"Good. Shall we proceed, then?"

"By all means. Let's have some action."

With a sweeping gesture, the Ringmaster brandishes his baton. The gem catches the light, winking. He dips smoothly, as if bowing, and thumps the baton against the floor. Two panels scroll open, revealing a spiral stairway that leads down into darkness. "Aha! I thought that would do it. Now, let's see if this answers some of our questions. After you, Miss Three."

As soon as the floor closes over them, I jump down from my hiding spot and book it out of there. But as fast as I run, I can't escape my fears. It's like someone took all those little doubts that have been cutting at me and turned them into a single horrible spear. I swear I can almost feel it, struck right through my heart.

I don't want to think about any of this, not about secret rooms or extreme measures or whether or not I belong in the new life I was promised. All I want is to find Nola and eat blue popcorn and watch some stupid mindless space opera. I can come back later to find out what's behind door number three.

CHAPTER 14

The Hasoo-Pashtung Bazaar

TURNS OUT "LATER" is an understatement. The midnight detour and the leech-bomb incident threw our schedule to bits, but now that we're getting back into settled space again, we've got a full roster of performances coming up. And that means practices and more practices, as well as costume design and fitting, prop and set prep, and a host of other details. Not to mention our normal share of schoolwork, courtesy of Miss Three and Core educational regulations. To be honest, I'm kind of relieved. It helps keep me distracted from the ache of all the questions and doubts I'm lugging around. Like what Miss Three meant when she said I didn't belong here. And whether Nyl might have been right.

Even if I weren't up to my ears in rehearsals and physics labs, it would be hard to unravel the mystery of the Restricted Area, because I can't find it. Five times I've gone out, retracing my steps. Once I ended up in the common room, and another time in the biohabitat. Once it was a room full of broken teapots. I tried to get my know-it-all to show me where it was, but the stupid thing refused, even when I threatened to melt it down and turn it into a potato peeler.

The Ringmaster is making himself pretty scarce lately, too. Sure, he'll wander into our classrooms and practice sessions now and then. Occasionally he'll take over, spinning the entire class off on a wild tangent about the taboo on eating fruit in public on Voxima-3. Or he'll have the Clown corps run through a scene in slow motion to "perfect the emotional tone." Some days I only realize he's watching by the weight of his stare. When I look up, he's already slipping out the door.

Then there was the time I was running down the hall late for Astrophysics and nearly bowled him over like I did the day we met. He twinkled that smile at me and said something silly about rabbits. I *wanted* to ask about the conversation I'd overheard. To trust the promise he made me. To find out the truth. But like a dork I stammered something about gamma radiation and ran away.

The truth is that I'm terrified. The truth is, I'm in love. With the Big Top, and with this life: the madcap antics of the other Clowns, Nola and her jokes and her kindness, the weird and wonderful meals Jom conjures from the culinary system, the stars swooping by over my bed at night. I can't bear the thought that someone might take that away. I love all of it too much.

Okay, not *all* of it. I don't think anyone could love the ridiculous costumes we Clowns have to wear for the Tree of Life act.

"It only makes sense. We're part of the Tree," says Theon. "It doesn't look *that* bad."

"Easy for you to say. You get to be a leaf. I look like I belong on Carmen Miranda's head." I prod one of dozens of puffy pear-shaped fruit decorating my green body suit.

"What? The translator didn't get that."

"Never mind." I sigh. "At least I get a cool costume for the Firedance."

Maybe I'm a little prejudiced, but the Firedance is going to be freaking *amazing*. We've been spending every day practicing for it, and I've put in a buttload of extra early-morning sessions. It's tougher than anything I've done before. The fact that I made up the choreography isn't much of a consolation, especially since I *still* haven't nailed the most important bit, that last throw-leap-catch, where I trick the King into kindling the seeds of the Tree of Life.

"How many people are going to be watching?" I ask, trying to ignore the knots that have taken up permanent residence in my stomach.

"Oh, it's only a mid-size show. Five thousand."

"For real? I'm going to be up there in front of five *thousand* people? Parading around with purple pears on my—"

"They're patching it into the local entertainment net, too," says Asha, from the cosmetics station, where she's testing out new makeup designs with her sister. "So there could be up to a hundred thousand watching the feed. Isn't that great?"

I open my mouth. No words come out. I can't breathe. Did my bodysuit suddenly get tighter?

"It's okay, Trix," Theon says. "You'll do fine. You've really been working hard."

"Not hard enough. The end of the Firedance—"

"Will be perfect. You've still got practice tomorrow morning."

I groan. "I need more. Maybe I could skip this bazaar thing and run through it a few more times this afternoon."

A chorus of protests slaps me down.

"You can't miss the Hasoo-Pashtung Bazaar," insists Asha, waving her airbrush.

Leri, one half of her face bright green, leans away from the mirror to tell me, "It's *amazing!* There's stuff there you can't get anywhere else in the universe! I found a set of antique Haitren dynasty beads last time."

"And a life-size hologram of Kel Starstrike," Asha adds. "*With* personalized audio." She pitches her voice low and dramatic. "*The universe is an empty void without you, my darling Leri. But you, my love, are the brightest star in*—mmmph!" She ducks as Leri directs one of the airbrushes at her, but not quickly enough to avoid a streak of orange across her cheek. Asha yowls and raises her own airbrush in retaliation.

"Hasoo-Pashtung really is something," says Theon, watching the antics of the sisters with a frown. "Hey, don't waste all the paint!" She returns her attention to me. "No one misses it. Everyone goes to the bazaar."

"What about the Ringmaster?"

Theon rolls her eyes. "Oh, no, he never leaves the Big Top. You'd think he was chained to it. But Miss Three has a mobile projection, to keep an eye on us."

"You mean to stop us from having any fun," says Asha. "First Tinker forbid we have a good time." The battle seems to have ended in a draw; both sisters are streaked in a clashing array of paints.

"To make sure we don't jeopardize the Circus," says Theon. "If the Core Governance starts sniffing around, they might find out what we really are. And if that happens, none of us is going to be having much fun ever again."

* * *

Nola and I meet up with Theon, Asha, and Leri inside the Big Top's main entrance for our escapade. The ship is parked in an assigned lot on the edge of the bazaar, the better to draw in crowds. With the doorways thrown open, a thousand scents and sounds flow into the Big Top. It's downright intoxicating, and I'm already glad I decided to take the break. This is my first chance to be on an actual alien world! We're weaving our way through the velvet ropes and pylons toward the door when someone speaks.

"Have a lovely time, ladies. Make the most of your freedom."

The Ringmaster leans against the ticket booth inside the doorway. With his features cast into shadow by the brim of his top hat, he seems oddly morose, even somber. Then he tilts his head, flashing white teeth. "And go ahead, get into a little trouble if you like. I won't tell Miss Three."

The other girls laugh and continue on. I pause a moment.

"Don't you want to see the bazaar?"

He drums thin fingers against his baton, silent. I get the impression he's trying out several answers in his head. "Oh, you know how it is," he says finally. "There's always something that needs looking after around here. And

I've seen bazaars before. I'll survive. Thank you," he adds, then waves to the door. "Better hurry on. Marvels to see, delights to sample. Be sure to try a sundae from Supulu's Stellar Scoops. Your mouth will be thanking you for the next year at least."

"Aliens have ice cream?"

"Everyone has ice cream. One of the very few things the Mandate got right."

"Okay, thanks for the tip." I start for the doors again, then stop. "Well, if you can't go, do you want anything? I mean, from the bazaar. Curried sardines?"

The Ringmaster chuckles. "Since you ask, I could use a good teapot. Never have found one that works quite properly. Always too big or too small, or worse yet, they dribble when you try to pour and you end up with stains all down your trousers." He gives a wan smile. How can the same person look so kindly one moment, and the next be "prepared to take extreme measures"?

"What's wrong?" he asks.

"You're just . . . confusing," I admit, startled into honesty.

"Well, I confuse myself sometimes, so that's no surprise. But Beatrix, is there something you want to ask?" He leans forward.

"I—" Questions hover on my lips. Then I catch sight of a shadow behind him. Miss Three. "Um . . . what's your favorite color? For the teapot."

"Today I'd have to say my favorite color is pink."
He winks. "Go on. Have fun."

I go, hurling myself into the chaos and wonder of the Hasoo-Pashtung Bazaar.

* * *

Two hours later, Nola and I duck under the lavender and green striped awning at Supulu's Stellar Scoops, bone-tired but over the moon with the wonder of it all. When I close my eyes, I can still see the dazzle of the light fountains. Scents of wood smoke and spun sugar and ozone cling to my skin. I've got a new pair of iridescent black boots, a freebie fiber-optic hair ornament some huckster shoved into my hands, telling me I was a "pretty pink lady," and a fuchsia teapot I haggled over for fifteen minutes. Silver ribbons stream down from my jacket, announcing my high scores at the gigantic Hasoo-Pashtung Arcade.

"It's just as well we're not old enough for the club," I say as I slide into a booth. I stretch my legs out. "My feet need a break, and my stomach needs ice cream."

"I guess," Nola says. She stands looking out across the street at Retrograde Station, bouncing slightly on her heels to the beat that we can feel even over here. "It's not fair. My birthday's next month! And I love dancing!" She spins around, gyrating to the distant music.

"Whoa. You've got moves." She does. I'm not just being nice. "Can't you, y'know, do your mojo to the ID station so it thinks you're older? Or someone else?"

"Oh, no! I mean, yes, I could try. But I wouldn't dare, not here. There's a Governance Guard on every corner, practically. And if I got caught . . ." Nola shivers.

"Next year, then. We'll get totally glammed." I dig in my bag for the hair extension and toss it across the table. "Then they'll see what they've been missing."

Nola clips on the glittering swatch of purple and models it with a snooty fashion-mag hauteur. Then we both dissolve into giggles.

"What should we get?" she asks, after we've recovered.

I study the tabletop, where a list of flavors scrolls by in a swirl of alien script my portable translator can barely keep up with. Every so often there's an advertisement showing a chubby redheaded toddler trying to stuff a giant ice cream cone into his mouth. "I can't tell what half this stuff is. How about we split one of these Asteroid Belt Blaster thingies? It's got a scoop of every flavor."

While Nola places our order, I check out the people hustling by on the street. It's freaky how human they look. The Mandate really did a number on the universe. Everywhere I look I see two eyes, ten fingers, two legs. But they've got differences, too, just like on Earth. They have skin, eyes, and hair of every color. Some folks have buck teeth or beaky noses, freckles or dimples. Others are rigged out in outlandish costumes, feathered head-dresses, and colorful tattoos.

A tall boy with a lumpy but genial face waves at me. I do a double take when I realize it's Gravalon Pree, his rocky features hidden by a holographic projection. Miss Three tried to get me to cloak my pink hair, but I refused. They've got hair dye in space, after all. It's funny, but I'm kind of attached to my bubblegum mop now. It's still my only proof that I'm anything out of the ordinary.

A whir of hydraulics pulls my attention back to the table as the robotic dessert cart trundles up with our order. Wielding a lobster-claw serving arm, the waitbot sets down a ginormous dish. A mountain of ice cream only slightly less impressive than Mount Everest rises up, its mottled colorful heights swathed in drifts of whipped cream and sprinkled with candied nuts.

I have to shift sideways to peer at Nola around the delicious monstrosity. "How many different flavors *are* there?"

Nola blinks wide eyes. "Forty-seven."

"I'm going to need a bigger stomach."

"I'm not even sure where to start," says Nola, her spoon hovering over the mountain.

"Tachyon Toffee Swirl, definitely. It's amazing." Jom slides into the booth beside Nola. He's wearing a wide, sombrero-like hat that I assume is intended to hide his bright red hair. His wraparound sunglasses, on the other hand, make him kind of dorky. "Hey, Nola," he says, smiling. "Looking good. Purple's my favorite color."

Nola flushes, raising one hand to the fiber-optic swatch.

Jom continues on, pointing out different scoops in the tower. "The Beta Berry Burst has a good flavor, but the texture's icy. Fudge Freefall is risky; if the under-chef did the fudge, it's brilliant, but if not, it's nasty. White Dwarf is the creamiest, but too bland. If it were me, I'd add a bit of tangelo zest. Radioactive Ripple and Dark Matter are pretty reliable. Definitely steer clear of the Cosmic Nut Crunch, though."

"Whoa. So I guess you eat here a lot," I say.

"Of course he does," says Nola, "his grand-mother—"

"Shh!" Jom cuts her off. "I'm incognito."

"Incognito?" I snicker. "In *that* get up?"

Jom pulls off the sunglasses. "Don't laugh. If the local management finds out who I am, they'll freak. It happens all the time."

"Find out what? That you're Ti—" I lower my voice. "I mean, that you're in the circus?"

"Worse," says Jom. He taps the tabletop as the advertisement with the ice-cream-slathered toddler scrolls by yet again. I look from the kid's scarlet curls to the bright red hair poking out from under Jom's hat.

"That's *you?*"

Jom sighs. "Good old Grandma Supulu. Why spend money on an actor when you can embarrass your own grandson in front of the entire universe?"

"You mean your grandmother *owns* this place?"

"This and 257,584 others. Normally I stay as far away as I can."

"So why are you here now?" Nola asks.

"Well . . . um . . ." A panicky look enters Jom's eye.

I nudge Nola's foot under the table. "Obviously he's here to save you from the evils of Cosmic Nut Crunch. The least you can do is thank him. Or maybe invite him to stay and help us eat this monster." Now if only Nola takes the hint. How such a smart girl can be so clueless is beyond me. Clearly Jom has one and only one reason for entering the confectionery danger zone. And if purple was really his favorite color before he sat down, then I'm the Wazeer of Deneb.

"Oh!" Nola flushes and sits up straight, shooting a sideways glance at Jom. "Trix is right. You have to help us with this thing. Which one did you say was the Beta Berry Burst?"

Under Jom's expert guidance we navigate the perils and delights of the Asteroid Belt Blaster. We sample scoops of every color and flavor imaginable (including a few that maybe should have stayed imaginary). But there's still at least half the mountain left when my stomach finally tells me enough is enough and that one more bite is going to bust my gut.

"I guess that's why they call it the Belt Blaster," I say, leaning back and groaning. "I can't believe I have to do backflips tomorrow." Then I catch sight of something that drives all my worries about tomorrow's performance away. "Is that Sirra?" I squint at the figure lurking in the alley across the street.

"Now *that's* how you go incognito," says Nola, giving Jom a meaningful look.

Incognito is right. I almost didn't recognize her in those drab brown coveralls with her hair stuffed under a gray cap. "What's she doing?"

"Maybe she wanted to find out how real people live," says Nola.

"Maybe she's got a secret boyfriend," says Jom. "Has to meet him on the sly."

"Looking like a street urchin?" I shake my head. "Huh. What's she got in her hand? Wait—she's headed into the alley now." I spring to my feet.

"You really care that much about Sirra's love life?" asks Jom.

"I'm coming, too," says Nola, sliding past Jom and out of the booth.

"Wait up, Nola!" calls Jom. "I can help—whoops! Sorry, ma'am, I didn't see you there. Stupid glasses. What? Um, yes, that's me, Jom Supulu. No, no, I'm only passing through. This isn't an official visit. *No,* I don't need any samples!"

I look back to see Jom fending off the advances of a woman who must be the store manager. Jom gives us a helpless wave as an army of lavender and green striped soda jerks whisk him off into the interior of the shop.

"Poor Jom!" says Nola with a giggle.

We head for the alley, skirting around the long line still queued up for entry to Retrograde Station. As we make our way along the passage, the dance beat thrums through the wall. From behind a large recycling bin, we watch as Sirra paces back and forth, down at the far end of the alley, beside what must be a back entrance to the club.

"What do you think she's waiting for?" asks Nola in a low voice.

"You mean who." I jerk my chin at the scene. A second figure slouches out of the shadows beyond Sirra. I can't make out his face under the dark cowl of his hood, but I think they're talking.

"I can't hear anything," I whisper, leaning closer, as if a few inches might reveal their conversation.

"She's handing him something. Looks like a bag. Wow. She does not look happy, though."

Sirra's hands flash like knives, cutting the air with angry gestures. Mr. Hoodie isn't impressed. He holds up a finger—no, two—then shakes his head.

Spinning on her heel, Sirra stalks away, continuing

down the alley. Mr. Hoodie watches until she reaches the far street. Then he heads up the stairs and into the club. The burst of music from the opened door dies away as it swings shut with a heavy thump, leaving Nola and me alone in the alley.

"Did you see his face?" I take the steps two at a time up to the door. I tap the panel but nothing happens. "Open up! Nola, we need to follow him."

"Trix, be careful!" Nola joins me on the landing, looking like she'd rather be anywhere else. "We can't break into Retrograde Station! Remember what I said? If we get caught, if we get noticed . . ."

"We won't get noticed. Come on, you can do it. You're a supergenius."

Nola gives a watered-down smile. "I don't know . . ."

"Please, Nola. Sirra's up to something. You know that. This is our chance to find out the truth!"

"Okay, I'll try." Nola closes her eyes for a moment, then raises her silver-palmed hand to the panel. She frowns, her lips twitching. "It's hard. I don't know if I can disable the protocols fast enough."

"You can!" I bounce on my heels, calculating how far the guy could have gotten by this time. "We've still got a shot at—"

The alarm shrieks across my words. Nola jerks back from the door, bashing into me. "Oh, no, no, no," she whispers. "I knew this was a mistake. We've got to get out of here. We can't get arrested. Hurry!"

We flee down the steps and start back along the alley. Too late. A pair of gray-capped Core soldiers pelt toward us. Both of them have stubby black rods pointed at us. "Halt and identify yourselves!"

Everything's falling apart, and all I can think is that it's my fault that Nola's here. I grab her hand, pulling her back the other way.

Nola stumbles. Her hand pulls free from mine. I look back in time to see her crumple, pressed to the ground like there's an invisible giant holding her there. She shrieks, pinned and helpless.

"Nola!" I beat at her invisible prison, but my fists bounce back. "Can you get yourself out?"

"I don't know. Oh, Trix, run! Get out of here. Please!"

"Not without you. There must be a way to break it. Maybe I can—"

"You're not going to do anything," snaps one of the guards, bringing her weapon up to point at me. The other guard still has his weapon trained on Nola.

I tighten my fists, my nails biting into my palms. After all the warnings about the Core, here I am about to get nabbed, and I've got Nola mixed up in it, too. I'm the worst roommate in the universe. The worst *friend* in the universe.

Maybe if I can take out the guy, bust that gizmo he's using, it'll free Nola. I'll take the fall, no question. Just please let Nola get away. I sink into a crouch, prepared to launch myself at him.

But someone else gets there first. It happens so easily, so quickly, that I don't have time even to blink before the two guards are on the ground.

Nola gasps, pushing herself to her knees. I scramble to her side, helping her up. Our rescuer drifts down from above like a slice of shadow.

"M-miss Three?" Nola stammers. "I—"

"'Thank you' would be the appropriate response." The simulacrum's voice sounds tinny, more distant out here in the street. "Perhaps followed by an apology for necessitating such extreme measures."

I look to the still bodies of the guards. "You didn't—"

"No, Miss Ling, they are not dead. Sadly that is not within my . . . mandate . . . to effect under the current situational parameters."

"So what now?" I ask.

"They will awaken shortly with headaches and a temporary blurriness of vision. I have already wiped all mobile data receptors and jammed local transmissions from this alley. Sadly they *will* retain their memories, so I suggest you remove yourselves and return to the Big Top. You've done enough to endanger the rest of the troupe already. I can only hope we will be able to prevent this from turning into a disaster."

CHAPTER 15

Break a Leg

B ACK ON THE BIG TOP, Nola and I spend the rest of the day waiting for the storm to hit, but nothing happens. And what with the million and one things we still need to do to get ready for the show, we don't have much time to obsess over it. Honestly, I'm a lot more worried about falling on my ass during the Firedance than about Miss Three's congenital pessimism.

By the next day the butterflies in my stomach have turned into a freaking plague of locusts, despite the fact that I finally nailed that tricky Firedance move during my morning practice. I sink down onto the red velvet carpet for the full-cast meeting and bend forward to stretch the stiffness from my hamstrings. I wish it were as easy to relax my nerves.

From the far side of the tent, Lorlyn, who does the music for the show, sends warm-up trills and odd high-pitched laughter across the empty stands. The lights high above twinkle as Toothy runs through a last set of tests. It's nearly showtime.

Nola plops down beside me, purple sparks glinting in her hair. I told her to keep the hair swatch. It looks cute on her. And it's not like I need more color. "Hey, Trix," she says. "Have you seen the Ringmaster? Did he say anything about yesterday?"

"No. Haven't seen him." I pull the sack beside me into my lap and double-check the contents. The teapot lies in pink splendor, remarkably uncracked despite yesterday's adventures. "Do you think he'll be mad?"

"He doesn't *look* mad." Nola nods to the doorway.

The Ringmaster strides to the center of the Ring, moving with a frenetic, almost manic energy. But Nola's right; he doesn't look angry. Distracted, maybe. The knot in my gut starts to relax, replaced by a fizzy feeling of excitement. I see it on the faces around me, too. We're like a soda given a good shaking, and we know the Ringmaster's about to open the bottle.

The chatter dies to silence as he searches the crowd,

his gaze catching each one of us in the net of his attention. "Ladies and gentlemen of the Circus Galacticus, this is it! There's a world out there waiting for you to wake up their hearts and dazzle their souls. You have worked hard, and I want you to know how deeply I appreciate that. You are all stars."

I don't usually go in for big speeches, but I have to admit it: Chills race up my spine. I'm not even that nervous anymore. I might be shaped like a girl, but I feel like a piece of lightning.

"Now, I have a few last-minute notes," he says, and begins reeling off a list of technical jargon. My attention drifts as he launches into a highly detailed discussion of the "emotional resonance" of Lorlyn's set piece, and how to work in some new thematic elements throughout the score for the show. I run through the Firedance choreography in my head, trying to remember the feel of landing the moves earlier that morning.

"And that leaves one last alteration," the Ringmaster is saying, "to the Firedance."

I jerk my attention back. Something about his voice sets me on edge. I realize I've got the teapot in a stranglehold.

"Due to some . . . technical difficulties, I've decided to return to the original Firedance choreography for this show. Beatrix, we can use your assistance backstage with the special effects. I trust Nola will be able to fill you in on that." He claps his hands, turning away. "All right, then! Time for the good luck circle. Gather round, everyone!"

"What?!"

It's not just me. A chorus of protests cuts across the room. Theon stands; Jom is waving his hands. But I'm the one the Ringmaster looks at when he finally faces us.

"You can't," I say. "Not after all the work I—we—put in. Do you think we're not good enough?"

"No, quite the opposite," he says, but his thin smile fades the next moment. "It's not that. It's what happened yesterday. We can't risk drawing the attention of the Core Governance."

"You want me to hide because I had a spat with some guards in an alley?"

"It was considerably more than a spat. If they recognized you and started asking questions, it would jeopardize the entire Circus. The Big Top is never more vulnerable than during a performance. Anyone can buy a ticket. Anyone can come in and see the show." He shakes his head. "I'm sorry, but Miss Three is right about this. In fact, it would be best if you remained behind the scenes completely. Especially with the additional danger of the Mandate attempting to—"

"Miss Three? This is *her* idea? So now you're letting her tell us what to do? I thought you didn't do that. I thought you wanted us to break out of our cages!"

The pain in his eyes kills me, but I'm too angry to stop now. If I hadn't gone into that damn alley in the first place, none of this would have happened.

"Beatrix, you have to understand—"

"Fine," I cut him off. "I get it." I spin around and head for the doors.

"Trix, wait!" Nola pelts after me.

I keep walking. "You heard him, Nola."

"But it's not like he's saying you're not good enough."

"Whatever. I've got to get out of here." I tear my eyes away from the circle gathering at the center of the tent.

"Trix, wait. It's tradition. We do the circle before every show, for luck."

"I don't need luck if I'm stuck doing some mindless behind-the-scenes garbage."

Nola looks at me with a stunned expression, like I disemboweled her favorite teddy bear.

"What?" I ask.

"That's what you think we Techs do? Mindless garbage?"

The catch in her voice stings me. I groan. "That's not what I mean, Nola. I think it's great that you're a Tech."

"Don't patronize me, Trix. I get enough of that already." Nola's voice breaks, recovers, breaks again. She turns around stiffly and heads for the crowd around the Ringmaster.

God, I'm screwing up *everything* I touch. I want to run after her, to explain, to make things right. But I can feel the tears burning in my eyes, and there's no way I'm letting anyone see them. I run out the door. Out in the hall I ditch the pink teapot in the nearest recycler. I never want to see that thing again.

* * *

I throw myself into the last-minute preparations. It's the best way to stop people from trying to talk to me. Don't get me wrong; I know they're trying to help. But I need work, not comfort. When the Ringmaster breezes through, I make myself scarce. There's no way I can speak to him without yelling, and that'll only make things worse.

What I do need is to apologize to Nola for putting my foot in my mouth so spectacularly. I have a pretty speech all worked out and everything. But there's no sign of her. Maybe she's doing some avoidance of her own. I wouldn't blame her.

The worst part isn't even that she might never want to see me again. I've been on my own, and it sucks, quite frankly. But I'd take that any day over hurting Nola, over making her doubt herself. My gut twists at the thought. Please let me have a chance to make this better.

Finally it's showtime. I lurk backstage, helping

Toothy with the special effects, trying not to look at the other Clowns out in the Ring. There's a special kind of pain in watching other people get something you want. It's not that I want them to fail, except maybe down in some deep nasty part of my self, a part I try to keep locked away.

I just . . . want it for me, too. And that feeling is like a hot razor slashing at my chest. I want the sweetness of the applause and the lights dazzling down and to know that I'm something bigger than my skin. I even want to be one of the stupid dancing fruit.

I thunk my forehead into the wall, running one hand back through my hair miserably. How pathetic am I?

"If you're going to sit here blubbering, I'd appreciate it if you'd shut me off again. Pity parties are *so* boring."

What the—? I feel for the know-it-all earpiece and realize I must have flicked it on accidentally. I'm about to shut it off, but a spark of outrage holds my hand back.

"Maybe I've got a good reason to be upset. Missing out on being a dancing fruit is one thing, but the Firedance was my big chance to . . ." I gulp.

"Show off?"

"No! To show what I'm capable of. To prove myself!"

"All you're proving right now is that you can pitch

a fit, dear. You'd never catch Dalana wallowing like this, letting her friends down because she suffered a disappointment."

"How exactly am I letting anyone down? The Ringmaster made it pretty clear they don't really need me."

"You're lucky I haven't got a corporeal form or you might have gotten your nose tweaked for that. How an otherwise clever girl could draw such a ridiculous conclusion is beyond me. Did you even try to understand the situation? No, of course not. Easier to be angry and upset than to do something productive."

"Are you calling me a coward?"

"What is that delightful phrase from your planet? If the shoe fits—"

I hit the "off" button. I so do not need this right now. But Britannica has one thing right. It's time to do something. The Tree of Life scene is just ending now. I still have a shot.

I find Jom and Theon and a couple of the other Clowns over by the costume racks. "You guys looked great out there," I say. "But you know what would really blow them away? Our Firedance. The new one."

Jom lifts his head. "Really?" I catch sparks of attention from some of the others, too.

"But we can't," says Asha.

"Yes, we can!" I say. "We've busted our asses getting ready for it, and a few Core nimrods aren't going to stop us. Don't you guys want this? Don't you want to show them what Clowns can do?"

There's a handful of cheers. And Jom, my hero, is already pulling out his fiery gauntlets and crown from a box behind a pile of stuffed fruit.

"But you can't go out there," protests Theon. "The Core guards might recognize you, like the Ringmaster said."

"Not if I look like someone else."

"How?"

I gesture around us. "This is the Circus Galacticus. We've got wigs, makeup, even freaking mobile image projectors. There's got to be a way."

"There is."

I turn to see Nola, standing with arms crossed, over by the makeup station. She doesn't look at me. "Jom, you guys better get that rustbucket off the staging lift and reset the floors for the new Firedance. I'll take care of Trix."

The rest of the Clowns dash off, buzzing with excitement. I *knew* they wanted this as much as I did. Only Theon is still frowning. Well, her and Nola.

Nola takes something out of her pocket, tapping at it with one silvery finger. It looks like the gizmo Gravalon Pree was using to go incognito in the bazaar. I can't believe she's actually helping me, after what I said.

I stop trying to remember my pretty speech. A jumble

of words spills out. "I'm sorry for what I said, Nola. I'm an idiot. I was upset, but I shouldn't have said that. I know you do an amazing amount of work for the show. Stuff I couldn't do if you sat me down for a year to teach me."

She sort of nods, her eyes fixed on the gadget.

"I'll make it up to you," I babble on. "I'll bribe Jom to make you Chocolate Supernovas every day. I'll do your chore section for the next month. I'll tattoo *Techs Rule!* on my forehead. But please, Nola, don't be mad. You're my best friend."

At that, she finally turns around to face me. She's biting her lip. "Okay," she says. "I'll forgive you. But only if you get the tattoo." Then she laughs, and everything is a million times better.

"I really will make it up to you," I say. "I promise."

"Well . . . I *am* scheduled to clear the auxiliary recycling system filters for my chore section this month. Nothing says 'I'm sorry' like slopping out trash for a friend."

"You got it." I try not to think too hard about what sort of disgusting things a spaceship full of teenagers can find to toss down the garbage chute.

"Here." She clips the image projector onto my belt, beside the bulge where I have the rock stuffed under my outfit. "I gave you brown hair, and—sorry—kind of a big nose. But no one should be able to tell it's you."

A series of thrilling chords booms out into the vastness of the tent. "That's your cue," Nola says. "I need to get back to the lighting booth. Good luck!"

As Nola heads off, I catch a glimpse of sequins. The Ringmaster. I duck around one of the screens, hiding out in the changing area until the coast is clear. I'm about to head over to my starting mark when Sirra comes around the corner, jostling into me.

"Watch where you're going," she snaps. "Some of us have to get ready to perf—" Sirra stops and stares at me. I realize she doesn't recognize me.

"Don't rush," I say, flicking off the image projector before she can start screaming about spies again. "Those folks are about to get blown away."

Her eyes widen. "I thought you were supposed to be backstage pushing buttons."

"Change of plans."

"Oh, really? Does the Ringmaster know about it?"

"He will in a moment." I consider a more violent response, but I've got more important things to do. Plus, Syzygy is standing over by the rack of spare costumes, repositioning one of the orange unitards between the reds and the yellows and carefully not watching us out of the side of her enormous glasses.

Sirra rolls her eyes. "Whatever. I have to get ready. The crowd will need some actual entertainment after they're done laughing you out of the Ring."

"Right," I say sarcastically. "Good luck."

Sirra continues on. I turn on the image projector again and check my reflection in the mirror. Man. That is one big schnoz.

"Break a leg," says Syzygy as I head on out to the Ring.

"What?"

She rearranges two shirts that both look blue-green to me and says, "It means good luck. In the idiom of your language. Is that not correct?"

"Yeah, I guess so," I say. "Good luck to you, too."

* * *

The Firedance is *amazing.* I'm talking write-it-in-the-sky, shout-it-from-the-mountaintops, utterly freaking amazing. We are on *fire.* Not literally, I mean, except for Jom as the King. But we smoke the house. They love us. They clap. They cheer. It's the sweetest thing I've ever heard.

It's *so* awesome, I'm pretty much in a daze by the time I dance offstage, the applause singing in my ears.

Something slams into me. An arm clamps across my chest; another grips my waist. Grinding breaths brush against my cheek. It's Nyl. The image projector crunches under his grip, and suddenly I'm back to my pink-haired self.

"Quite a performance, Beatrix," he says. "Maybe

you do belong here. But I can't allow you to jeopardize everything we've worked for."

I kick out, but my feet only catch the hem of his long coat. His cold hand slides along my waist. Something rips. Air whispers against my skin. He pulls away, holding something.

I brush my fingers over my side, feeling for the injury, but there's nothing, not even a cut. It's a more terrible wound than that. He's got the rock.

Grabbing hold of one of the costume racks, I drive it across the floor toward Nyl. It catches him in the chest, slamming him back into the special-effects station. Metal crunches. Something sizzles. I smell burnt plastic.

Nyl pulls himself up, tearing free a half-dozen hoses from the FX station. They hiss puffs of artificial smoke into the air between us. He runs.

I hurl myself upright and take off after him. He's heading for the emergency exit. I shout, the words garbled by rage and desperation. I put all my energy into one last lunge.

Nyl swivels toward me as I leap. My hands lock into fists. He flicks something into the air between us. I catch one last glimpse of that mask before blue fire webs lace across my vision, dragging me down to the ground. I scream. The physical agony is nothing compared to what I've lost. How could I let this happen?

Lorlyn's soaring voice fills the Big Top, mocking my

loss with a song of triumph and victory. As I stare wildly up, I see two silver figures flying among the clouds.

Not clouds. Smoke. Billows of it jet upward from the busted mess of the special-effects station. Sirra flips out into the void, just as a great gust of smoke hits. Then she's lost in it. All I can see is Etander, hanging from his own trapeze, arms out to catch her.

The music is too loud. I can't hear his shout, but I see it: his lips pulling back, his sudden jerkiness as he reaches for something that isn't there.

A single silver arrow plummets from the clouds like a fallen angel, already limp as a rag doll. Did she hit something? Get knocked out by the smoke? My finger-nails dig into my palms as I scream for her to wake up and save herself.

The vibration of the impact ripples through the flooring, sending an answering tremor through my body. The music stutters out, punctuated by cries from the stands. Somewhere above I hear Etander shouting his sister's name, but the huddle of silver in the center of the Ring doesn't move.

CHAPTER 16

Fairy Tales

AT BREAKFAST the next morning, I slump into one of the seats at the fifth table. Life moves on around me. The Clowns chatter and joke, the Techs visit their virtual world, the Principals lounge and preen. The Freaks are playing some sort of board game with armies of little toy soldiers. I'm still stuck in yesterday, my mistakes on infinite repeat in my head. I haven't slept, and my mouth fills with sawdust at the thought of food.

"You should go back to the Tech table," I tell Nola. "*You* didn't send Sirra to the infirmary with a broken leg and a concussion, saddle the Ringmaster with a ginor-mous fine, and lose the one thing your dead parents told you to keep safe. I deserve to be exiled so I can wallow in my guilt. You don't."

"Oh, go right ahead and wallow," Nola says with a sly look. "I'm here because I need room to clean out my toolbox."

I can believe it. By the time she's dumped every-thing out, there's at least three dozen gizmos, gadgets, and doodads laid out on the table between the bowl of fruit and the platter of pancakes. I shake my head at the now-empty toolbox in Nola's lap, which is about as big as a textbook. "I don't see how it all fits. Unless that thing is bigger on the inside than the outside."

"Give me a few years and maybe I'll figure out di-mensional transcendence. For now it's all about organi-zation. Everything has a place." She slides a small wrench into one corner of the lid.

"Yeah," I say. "Right."

Nola looks up sharply. "Trix. You have a place. You're still a Clown."

"They all hate me. You should have seen the look I got from Theon. Urrgh." I slice one of the muffins in half, then in halves again.

Nola spins the screwdriver she's been cleaning between her fingers. "Did they *tell* you not to sit with them?"

"No," I admit. "But I don't deserve to sit there. It's all my fault this happened."

There's enough of a pause that I know I'm right. Nola clears her throat. "When the Ringmaster is done smoothing things over with the Hasoo-Pashtung authorities, I'm sure he'll figure out a way to—"

"It's not his problem to fix," I say. "Enough with the wallowing." I shove my diced muffin down the recycler. Across the room, Etander is sitting quietly at the Principals' table. Maybe I shouldn't bother him. I might rile him up into Hedgehog Boy, talking about the accident.

It's a nice excuse, all thoughtful on the surface. And all cowardice underneath. No, I've got to do this. I leave Nola to finish organizing her toolbox. She looks up with worried eyes. "Are you sure you don't want me there for moral support?"

"Thanks, but groveling goes better without moral support." I draw in a breath and head for the Principals' table.

They all look at me, except Etander. He stares into his empty plate like it's a crystal ball. "Hey, Etander," I begin. Man, my voice sounds creaky. I cough. "I wanted to apologize for screwing up the smoke machine thing."

He looks at me then, and I kind of wish he hadn't. It's not an accusing or angry look, but it still makes me feel about an inch tall. I'm a pathetic worm. He gives a small nod but says nothing.

"I swear it was an accident."

"I believe you," he says finally. "But I'm not the one you should be apologizing to."

Ouch. All right, I deserved that. I mumble something and start to walk away, then stop. "Sirra's still in the infirmary, right?"

Etander nods. "Miss Three said it would be another day before the bone had regenerated enough for her to risk moving around, even using her powers."

"Okay. Thanks."

I practically run from the cafeteria. Nola catches up with me in the hall outside. "Trix, where are you going?"

"To do more groveling."

She falls in step with me. "Don't worry; I'm not here for moral support. I figure someone better be there in case she goes for your head. Plus, you'll get lost otherwise, since you still refuse to be sensible and use your know-it-all."

"I remember the way. Mostly," I add as Nola grabs my elbow to redirect me at the next junction.

A few minutes later we're standing outside a door marked with the linked-hands symbol that's apparently the intergalactic version of the Red Cross. Nola is about to touch the entry pad when I motion for her to stop. "I hear voices. She's talking to someone."

"So?"

"I don't want to grovel in front of Miss Three. Or the Ringmaster."

"And I thought you were supposed to be brave,"

Nola says teasingly. "Don't worry; it's not either of them. Can't you hear the static? That's some sort of audio feed. Probably her parents checking in on her. It was all over the news about the accident."

Sirra's voice suddenly rises in volume, so that every word rings clearly even through the door: "—you hateful, manipulative bastards! I did what you asked! Leave us alone!"

Nola winces. "Maybe she doesn't get along with her folks?"

"Or maybe it's not her parents."

The conversation seems to be over. Someone's moving around inside. I lean toward the door to listen, only to have it slide open under my palms, sending me tumbling into the room.

I guess if I'm going to grovel to a girl who hated me even before I broke her leg, falling flat on my face is a good way to start. Nola gives me a cheery wave as the door skims shut, leaving me alone with Sirra.

She looks less like an invalid and more like somebody caught in the act of doing something she shouldn't. The hem of her black nightgown drifts around her knees, revealing one normal leg and one that's covered in a layer of something resembling marshmallow fluff. Her hands are tucked behind her, and she's pressed herself back against the wall. Neither of us says anything, but I hear a distant rattle and a click. Did she throw something down the recycler chute?

By the time I've got myself vertical again, Sirra's back in her bed, the viewscreen of her know-it-all covering one eye. Huh. She's ignoring me completely. I'd have thought she'd be enjoying this.

I clear my throat. "I'm sorry I messed up your act," I say, shoving the words out. "And that you got hurt."

She gives a little shrug, like I'm a fly buzzing in her ear. "Sure. Whatever."

Something's definitely wrong. I was sure she'd have me licking her boots by this time. "Okay, then." I head for the door.

"Trix."

I stop. Here it comes. "Yeah?"

"Is Nola out there?"

"Um. Yeah. Why?" Maybe she wants to ream me out in front of an audience? Okay, if that's what it takes.

Sirra opens her mouth, then snaps it shut. "Never mind. Go on. Try not to break any of *her* bones."

Honestly, I'm kind of relieved when she says that. For a minute there I was afraid the fall busted more than her leg. But this is the Sirra I know and don't love.

Once I'm out in the hall, I fill Nola in. "Weird, huh? I'm still not even sure she noticed me apologizing."

"She has been acting pretty strange lately, making all those mystery calls off-ship. I wonder . . ."

"What?"

"Well, you said she saw you getting ready for the

Firedance. She knew what you'd look like, even with the image projector. So I'm wondering if maybe . . ."

"She tipped off Nyl?" I lean back against the wall as it all clicks into place. "Nola, you're brilliant."

She grins, but her smile fades after a moment. "But Trix, that's horrible. To think she'd sell us all out. I mean, she's one of us. She needs the Circus as much as anybody. It can't be true."

"I dunno." I shake my head. "Her family has money and power. That can hide a lot of dirty laundry. Plus it's not like she's got three eyes or antennae or pink hair. Sirra can pass for normal."

"But Etander can't."

"Yeah." I shake my head. "The Tinkers sure handed out some crazy gifts, didn't they? I mean, what's the point of turning into a porcupine like that? Or pink hair, for that matter?"

Nola shrugs. "Maybe there is no point. This is the Tinkers we're talking about, after all. Who knows if they were trying to do any of this? Your pink hair, my tech-interfacing, it could be intentional or it could be recycled bits of old lab experiments."

Recycled. "I think Sirra was throwing something in the recycler, right when I came in. If we could find it, maybe we could figure out what she's up to."

Nola frowns thoughtfully. "The reclamation system will be down for the filter cleaning, so whatever she threw away will still be in the tanks until tonight. But Trix, we don't even know what we're looking for. And the Big Top makes a *lot* of trash. I can only think of one way this might work."

"What?" I ask. Nola looks suddenly queasy, like she just came back from a long spacewings flight.

"We'll have to convince Rjool to help us."

"Rjool? Is he one of the Freaks?"

"No, Rjool isn't Tinker-touched. He isn't even . . . well, you'll have to see for yourself. He never leaves the engineering zones. Oh, I really wish there was another way."

"Why? What's wrong with him?"

Nola opens her mouth, but before she can say more, we both become aware of footsteps approaching.

The Ringmaster comes around the corner and halts at the sight of us. "Ah. Beatrix. Good. Nola, if you'll excuse us?"

I fight the urge to grab Nola's arm and cling to her like a life preserver. The Ringmaster doesn't actually look angry. But he does look serious, and there are shadows under his eyes.

I wave Nola off. "Meet you after lunch for chore section." Then I'm alone with the Ringmaster. He has his hands shoved into his pockets, his chin tucked down into his collar.

All my mistakes hang in the air between us. The

silence goes on long after Nola's footsteps have faded. The words finally burst out of me. "Aren't you going to yell? Ream me out for being such an idiot and nearly getting Sirra killed? Not to mention losing the ancient Tinker artifact?"

"No," he says. "You aren't the only one who's made mistakes. There are things you need—" He falters. "Things I need to tell you."

"Is this about the rock?"

He hesitates. "In part. But I think this conversation would benefit from a change in venue."

I follow him silently down the hall and along several others. We don't talk. I hate this feeling, like I'm headed off to take a test I didn't study for. And there's no more time to cram. Do or die.

It's a relief when we finally get to the viewing deck. The Ringmaster walks slowly to the windows and sets his elbows on the railing, staring out into space. I clear my throat. "You're not going to tell me the rock is dangerous, are you? I mean, Nyl said it was. But he's one of the Mandate, so that's just a bunch of bad-guy talk, right? I mean, it's not true. He was trying to scare me."

The Ringmaster turns his back to the stars, locking me in place with his gaze. "A villain can speak the truth as well as any hero. Perhaps better. There are truths that can be hard to hear. Things you might not want to believe."

I have a nasty feeling there's a pit about to open

up under my feet. "You know something you're not telling me."

"Oh, many things, no doubt. Would you like to know the secret ingredient in Tachyon Toffee Swirl? The last words of the Hermit of Pergola-7? The absolutely best place in the universe to have a spot of tea?"

I try to smile but fail. "I want to hear about the rock. You found out what it is, didn't you?"

"I have . . . an educated guess." He pauses. "Did your parents tell you fairy tales?"

"Huh?"

"Bedtime stories, old legends of faraway places? Heroes and quests and curses?"

"My dad learned all sorts of crazy folktales from his grandma. Frogs trapped in wells and monkey kings leaping across the clouds. They always made him sad, though." I hadn't understood why, back then. Now I blink my eyes and wonder if the Ringmaster can see that same look in my face. I cast my mind back through layers of tears and bleakness to happier times. "My favorites were these amazing stories he made up about aliens. I figured out later that he stole half the plots from old movies, but I loved them so much it didn't matter. Reaching the stars was my happily-ever-after." I shake my head. "What do fairy tales have to do with my rock?"

"Let me tell *you* a fairy tale, Beatrix, and see what you make of it. Some of it Miss Three recovered only recently, from the datastore fragments we found on the Lighthouse. Some I already knew. Some may truly be only a fairy tale." He clears his throat, then begins in something closer to his stage voice.

"Once upon a time there were two powers, the Mandate and the Tinkers. They battled each other in word and deed, both convinced they knew what was best for the universe. Great and terrible were their battles as they warred across the universe. But in time, each faded, drained by the endless conflict. And eventually they disappeared. Some say they died out. Others whisper that they will return one day, to wage their battles anew. All we know for sure is that they left behind their children, raw and inexperienced, to forge a new world from the ashes. And they left an inheritance: of technology, of ships, of gifts hidden in the blood and bones of the new generations.

"But the greatest treasures—their greatest weapons—they hid away in secret. Perhaps to await their own return. Perhaps to await future generations wise enough to use them."

I can't help interrupting. "Weapons? What kind of weapons?"

The Ringmaster drops his storytelling air to give a bemused sigh. "It's an old, old story, worn with time and translation. All we have left are the names and a handful of maddeningly vague details. The Mandate's Treasure is called the Cleansing Fire. I will leave it to your imagination to consider the implications of that delightful name."

"And the Tinkers' Treasure?"

"The oldest stories call it the Seed of Rebirth. They say it holds the essence of the Tinkers' Touch. A power that can reshape a living being, granting it new abilities, new life, whatever it needs to evolve and grow. The pinnacle of their genetic technology."

I have a horrible suspicion of where he's going with this. "And the maddeningly vague details? Let me guess. It's a shiny black stone."

He gives a faint sad smile and taps his nose.

"My rock. You're saying my rock is the Tinkers' Treasure."

"Yes."

"And now the Mandate has it. Because I couldn't keep it safe." I sag against the railing. "How did my parents get their hands on something like that? A pair of scientists on some podunk planet in the Exclusion Zone just happened to find an ancient alien treasure?"

"Your parents were more than that."

"So they *were* Tinker-touched? Right? That must be it."

The Ringmaster is silent for so long I start to quiver. I want to pace, but I refuse to walk away. I have to see his face when he says what's coming.

213 ✡

"Once upon a time," he begins, "there was young woman, the daughter of an ancient household of great power. This young woman saw much of the ways of her kinfolk, and did not like them. She wished to walk another path. Then a day came when her people captured a grand prize, the greatest treasure of their enemies, bought with blood and death and pain. Terrible pain . . ."

"Ringmaster?"

He shakes himself, continuing on. "The girl's people threw a grand celebration. They held the future of their enemy in their hands, and they planned to crush it. To destroy it.

"But the girl had already looked upon the treasure and seen its beauty. She could not let it be destroyed, even if it meant defying her family, her blood. So she stole the treasure and ran far, far away. She found a world that knew nothing of her kind, a place where she herself was a fairy tale. And she met a young man who had stars in his eyes. She shared her secret. They fell in love. They had a daughter." He looks at me.

"No. Freaking. Way. My mom was one of the Mandate?"

The Ringmaster eyes me quizzically. "I'll admit to taking some artistic license in the telling of the tale, but between what you've told me and what I've gathered, I believe it's true."

My feet carry me back and forth along the viewing deck, beating into the metal flooring with a reliable, sensible *thunk, thunk, thunk.* It's about the only thing in my life that is reliable or sensible right now.

"How did I get through the mirror?" I say suddenly, seizing on the first of the hundred questions fogging my brain. "The only reason my hair turned pink was that rock. Right?"

"We don't know that," says the Ringmaster, but the doubt in his voice punches me in the gut. "It could be that you inherited the genetic markers from your father. And even if it is the result of the Seed, what does it matter? You still bear the Tinkers' touch."

"It matters because I don't really *belong* here." My voice is so sharp now I half expect my lips to bleed. "That's why Miss Three said I was a danger."

"When did Miss Three say you were a danger?"

I halt, crossing my arms. "When you two were in the Restricted Area talking about using 'extreme measures.'"

"Ah. That." The Ringmaster gives the jeweled top of his baton an unnecessary polish. "Miss Three is truly one of a kind. Or three of a kind, to be perfectly accurate. I trust her opinions on a great many things. But where you're concerned, she's hardly an impartial judge. Please believe me when I say that I do not, and never have, believed you to be the enemy, no matter your parentage. And I blame myself for not telling you the truth sooner. I thought . . . I was afraid it might hurt you. That it would make you doubt yourself."

"You were right." I press my palms to my temples.

My skull feels heavy, stuffed with iron and nails. I run my fingers back through my hair, gripping handfuls. My scalp prickles with pain. "Talk about fairy tales. Here I was, believing I was one of the superheroes, that some ancient power chose me to do great things. But I'm one of the bad guys." A bitter laugh spills out of me.

"Beatrix, I—"

"No! No more lies." My voice cracks. The tears start to leak through. I grab hold of the railing to keep me strong. "You told me I was special. You made me believe it, even when I flunked all the tests. You handed me a dream, even though you knew it was a lie."

"But you are—"

"Don't you dare say it!" I rip my hand away from the barest brush of his fingers. "Don't you dare lie to me again. I can't take it. Really. I try to be tough and all that, but this is too much. I'm in too many pieces. You can't wave your baton and dance them all back together again like that."

I don't bother brushing the tears from my eyes anymore. I run, leaving the Ringmaster and his false dreams where they belong, with the stars that are always going to be beyond my reach.

CHAPTER 17

Rjool

THE NEXT FOUR HOURS ARE TORTURE. The Ringmaster's fairy tales grow sharp claws and tear my thoughts apart. There's no way I'm going to Miss Three's lecture on Core Governance Trade Law, or even the symposium one of the older Techs is giving on Strong and Weak Nuclear Forces. I go to the common room instead and run myself through the Arena at level eleven. Maybe if I can squeeze all the sweat from my body, there'll be nothing left to feed my tears. On my seventh run I make it five minutes, a new personal record.

But the truth of who I am turns the victory as hollow as my stomach.

I grab what I can from the vending machines on the way back to the dorms rather than face lunch in the cafeteria. I'm not a coward, I'm . . . establishing a defensive position. Marshaling my resources for a big comeback performance.

Yeah, I don't really believe it, either. But it's a lie I need right now.

Back in the dorm, I mechanically down a half-dozen energy bars and protein drinks. My stomach rebels at first, but I keep going. I'm going to need my strength to get the Tinkers' Treasure back.

It's my only choice, really. It's not like I'm going to run off and sign up with the Mandate, no matter who Mom was. And sure, I could hightail it back to Earth, make some sort of lame life for myself. It's probably where I belong, but I can't leave yet, no matter how much I want to get away from everything that reminds me of my broken dream. The Big Top may not be my place anymore, but I can't leave it like this, suffering for my mistake. And the next step to finding the Tinkers' Treasure is figuring out what Sirra is up to.

By the time Nola comes in, I'm practically bouncing off the walls between the sugar and my need to do something constructive. Or destructive.

"Trix," she starts off, "have you been hiding in here

all—what's wrong?" She steps closer, looking way too intently into my eyes. "Have you been crying? What did the Ringmaster say?"

"It doesn't matter," I say, bounding upright and starting to sweep up the layer of wrappers and drink cartons from the bed.

"Are you sure?"

"He found out what the rock was," I admit. "He called it the Tinkers' Treasure."

Nola gapes for a moment. "As in, the long-lost artifact that holds all the secrets of the original Tinkers?"

"That's the one. So it's pretty much the last thing you'd ever want the Mandate to get their hands on. Basically, I screwed up royally, and we need to get it back before they destroy it. Please tell me this Rjool character is going to need a butt-kicking. I am crazy-ready to thwack something."

"That'll be hard, since Rjool doesn't have a . . . well, you'd have to find something else to kick. Here, I brought gear." She tosses me a set of yellow coveralls and a pair of rubbery black gloves. "But we don't want to fight him. He's a Loranze."

"A what?" Following Nola's lead, I pull on the coveralls over my clothing, relieved to finally be doing something. Even if I don't get to thwack anything.

"Ask your know-it-all to show you."

"Oh, my stars," says Britannica when I put the question to her. "A Loranze? That won't do, not at all. Nice young ladies shouldn't be associating with creatures like that."

"No worries for me, then."

My know-it-all tsks me. "I admit that you're a work in progress, dear, but there's potential. So it would be highly unfortunate for you to be fraternizing with one of the Untouched."

"The Untouched?"

"One of the very few races in all the universe not tampered with by the Mandate or the Tinkers. Highly dubious characters, in my opinion. Look."

The viewscreen slides out over my eye. I nearly jump out of my big yellow boots. "Whoa. Now, that's what I call an alien."

Hovering in front of me is the frozen image of something that looks like it belongs on one of those nature programs about deep-sea critters. "Are those tentacles? But those numbers can't be right. Average weight five tons? Average height fifty feet? How did something that big get in here?"

As we make our way to the engineering sector, Nola fills me in. "You can mail-order Loranzelli eggs over the universal net. They come with a tank and everything. It's a big gimmicky thing, and half the eggs don't even hatch, and the other half aren't even real Loranzelli, just some sort of genetically altered cephalopods. The rumor is somebody on the Big Top got a real one, and when they realized it, they tossed it down the recycler. By the time they found Rjool, he was too big to get out easily. No one's ever admitted to being the one who tossed him, though."

We're headed through an unfamiliar part of the ship now. The halls are narrower, and half the doors are plastered with dire warnings about electrocution, radiation, and cataclysmic polarity reversal.

"Anyway," she goes on, "Rjool does a good job keeping the recyclers running. He can handle everything except the one set of auxiliary filters that's on the other end of the recycling zone, and we have those in chore rotation. I've spent about five minutes, tops, down here in the past month, now that he's taken over the water reclamation system, too. But believe me, five minutes is more than enough."

"So he *is* dangerous?"

"Well, in a way. He likes to talk, and ask questions. Personal questions."

"So, like, he wants to know your favorite color? How does that qualify as dangerous?"

"I'm serious," Nola says. "You won't be laughing five minutes from now. He knows things about all of us from going through the trash. It's like he can read your mind, like he knows all your worst secrets. You step one toe into his lair, and the next thing you know he's pulling out a dirty sock and asking you about the fight you had with your mother last Tuesday. It's amazing. Well, repulsive and amazing." She pauses in front of a large door. "Ready to see for yourself?"

I am suddenly way less interested in meeting Rjool. All my worst secrets? But I need to find that rock. I sigh. "Are you sure we can't just kick his—tentacles—and make him help us?"

Nola opens the door.

"Never mind," I say. Because by then, I've seen Rjool. He's hard to miss, since he fills up at least half the room. It reminds me of the banyan tree I saw once on a nature special. It looked like a huge grove of small trees, but it was really this one massive tree with all these weird roots dripping off it.

Rjool is like that, except the trunk in the center has five globby eyes and a clattering beaky mouth, and the things dripping out of the air everywhere are tentacles, not roots. They *slither.* If you can imagine a room with snakes plastered over every bit of floor and wall, you can get how creepy this place is.

Two of the eyes turn in our direction. There's not a lot of space left that isn't full of whispering tentacles, but Nola finds us a bare spot near the center of the room. A hollow, boomy voice fills the room.

"Noooooola. How good to see you again. How is the new skin treatment? Taking care of all that pesky acne?"

A thin tentacle wriggles forward, holding an empty jar emblazoned with the animated face of a boy peppered with zits that shrink as he lathers on a blue goop.

"Yes," says Nola in a tiny voice. She looks ready to melt into the flooring.

"And what about that other new cosmetic cream? I know I have the bottle here somewhere . . ." Tentacles slither around us. Nola gives a low moan. "You know the one," he continues. "The label says it will increase the—"

"Hey," I interrupt. "Do the words *not your business* exist in your language or what?"

Three of Rjool's eyes turn to ogle me. "And you've brought me someone new. Mmmmm . . ."

I'm no expert on reading the expressions of banyan tree–squid aliens, but I think he's looking at me like I'm something good to eat.

"We're here to clean the filters," says Nola, rallying herself. "And to ask a favor."

"A favor? *Hooohooohoooo . . .*"

I realize after a moment that he's laughing. It makes all the tentacles shiver. And me.

"There are no favors," says Rjool. "But introduce me to your friend. I looove meeting new people." He clatters his beak.

"I'm Trix," I say, "and we need to get whatever it was Sirra ditched in the infirmary recycling system this morning. And that's all you need to know."

"Oh, ho . . . It sounds as if someone has something to hide. A few sordid little secrets, hmmm?" Now all five eyes are staring at me, like they can see right into my soul. Or worse, into my DNA.

I shake myself. Rjool couldn't possibly know about my parents. Even *I* didn't know until today. He's playing me. "Listen, you overgrown squid, this is important. There might be a Mandate spy on the ship, and this is evidence."

"You care a great deal about this ship, considering you've only lived here for six weeks. Aren't you afraid to love something so much? What if you lose it?"

Nola steps in, which is good, because I swear I'm about to start tearing off tentacles. "Okay, Rjool," she says, "you know what we want. So are you going to help or not?"

Two large tentacles twist forward across the trunk, like crossed arms. "I can find your evidence. But first, your friend will answer three questions."

"What kind of questions?" I demand.

Rjool waves three small tentacles in the air around me. "Interesting. Your pulse rate has increased considerably since you first entered my domain."

"Fine. I'm not scared of you, or your questions. I just don't want to waste any more time."

"Trix, you don't have to do it. I can find something to bribe him with," says Nola, lowering her voice. "I'll offer him my signed poster of the twins. He's a huge fan of *Love Among the Stars*."

"No, we're here now, and we need that clue. I'll do it."

"Oh, gooood," says Rjool, clapping two tentacles together. A shiver runs through the rest of the snaky mass. "Now, let me see what I have here. Ah, yes, that's a good starting point." A tentacle curls out, holding a ragged piece of cloth embroidered with a golden letter *B*. "Tell me about this . . ."

I lick my dry lips. "It's the insignia from my old school. Bleeker Academy."

"It was the very first thing to come through the system bearing traces of your genetic material. "Why were you in such a hurry to throw it away?"

"It was coming loose, anyway."

"But some of these threads were cut. You went to the effort of removing it."

"Okay, fine, I cut it off. I'm done with that place, with Primwell and the rest of them. It was a nasty, horrible cesspool of a school. And I am not going back. I'd rather get pitched into a black hole."

"You aren't planning to stay on the Big Top, then?"

"I can't—"

Nola's expression freezes the words on my lips. I switch gears. "Is that another question?"

"Only if you want it to be," Rjool says in a voice that runs over my skin like oil.

"Give me another, then. Let's get this over with."

Rjool rumbles with laughter. Creep. "Here's a promising little trinket," he says. Something sails toward us along the sea of tentacles, bobbing like a round, hot-pink boat.

"Trix, that's the teapot you got for the Ringmaster. But you worked so hard bargaining for it! Why did you throw it out?"

"Yes, Trix, why?" echoes Rjool.

"It's broken. Look—the handle has a big chip in it."

"Mmm-hmmm, yes." Rjool nods, and I think I'm off the hook until he adds, "But that chip came from rough contact with the recycling system filters. In other words, after you threw it away. If you want my help, stop lying and answer my question."

"Why do you care? What's it matter to you?"

"I simply find it intriguing that someone would go to the effort of acquiring an object so calculated to please a particular someone, and then immediately throw it away. It bespeaks a troubled relationship, veering from intense friendship to petulant rage."

"I am *not* petulant," I snap. "He lied to me! He made me believe—"

"Yes?"

"That's your answer," I say. "That's what you get. You want more, make it question number three."

"Very well. I think you've made it clear. That leaves one question." Rjool's eyes quiver, all five of them goggling at me like I'm a freaking science experiment. "It so happens that an odd recycling deposit came down from the infirmary earlier today. The dusting of skin cells I took matches the genetic signature of Sirra Centaurus." He holds something in one loop of tentacle, but it's so small I can't make out what it is.

"So you've got what we want. Give me the question already."

"You're very eager to prove she's the spy. Why is that?"

"That's a no-brainer. Of course I want to find out who's feeding information to the Mandate. You remember them, right? The enemy who wants to destroy us all?"

"But you seem *particularly* eager to prove that Sirra is the spy. You're even willing to go through her garbage to do it." He brandishes the thing in his tentacle. "This could be something perfectly harmless. It could even be quite personal. And yet you're prepared to sweep that all aside to indulge your own curiosity. Maybe what I should be asking is whether the words *not your business* exist in *your* language."

"It's not the same thing!"

"Isn't it? Please, explain . . ."

"It's—Well, at least I'm trying to keep this ship safe. You're doing it for kicks."

"But you would be happy if you could prove Sirra was the spy, wouldn't you?"

I bat aside a tentacle as it tries to slide up along my arm. "Okay, yes! Maybe because then I don't need to feel so guilty for landing her in the infirmary. There, you've got it, proof I'm a rotten person. Happy now?"

"Yes, this is quite stimulating. Much more entertaining than the usual games. But I still need the truth."

"She's just so—" I clamp down on the words, holding them in. Oh, Rjool is clever all right.

"Perfect?" he finishes. "You can't stand to see someone shining so brightly, when you're worried your own light is only a reflection."

I open my mouth to protest, already shaking my head. "Yes." The word slips out before I can catch it and stuff it back deep inside.

"Hmmmmmm . . ." is all Rjool says.

I draw a long breath, trembling with adrenaline. Remember the mission, I chant to myself, curling and uncurling my fists.

"Okay," says Nola abruptly, "that's three. We're done. Hand over the clue, Rjool."

A single tentacle slips forward to drop a small nub of metal and plastic into her outstretched hand. "A pleasure, Trix, Nola. Do come again."

I force myself not to run from the room under those five goggly eyes. Out in the corridor I let myself sink against the wall. I'm shaking even worse now. Nola's looking at me like I'm some broken gadget she doesn't know how to fix.

"I'm okay," I say. "Is he always that twisted?"

"I guess it's the only entertainment he's got, stuck down here. But Trix, are you *really* okay? Do you need to . . . talk about anything?"

"No!" I wince. "Sorry, didn't mean to shout. But the last thing I want right now is more talking. Let's see if it was worth it. Is that a datastore?"

"Looks like one." Nola searches the wall with a slight frown. "Need to find a port, and we can see what's on it. There's one, down that way."

We head back along the corridor. Nola taps the wall, revealing a screen, keypad, and various other mysterious buttons and lights. "Ready?" She looks to me, holding the datastore up, ready to plug it into one of the sockets.

I nod. "Let's see what Sirra's been hiding."

"Huh. It looks like a bunch of medical files."

Images begin flipping across the screen. They look like EKGs and MRIs and all those other funky medical acronyms. Then I spot an X-ray of a hand, with a shadowy overlay of spikes along the back, and recognize it, even before we get to the videos of his face. Etander, smooth-skinned and gorgeous, changing to Etander, tormented and bristling with spines.

"What *is* this?"

Nola shakes her head. "There's a pre-recorded videostream. Here, I'll play it."

The gray static clears to an image of a man's face, hidden by a featureless mask. When he speaks, his voice is deep and oddly off-kilter. "We're disappointed, Miss Centaurus. We thought you understood our position and were prepared to deal seriously with us. But you have not delivered the promised payment in full. You know what is at stake. Do you want the entire Core to learn the truth about your brother? If you value your mother's position and the reputation of your family, you will transmit the remaining funds at once. You have one week, or we release the files."

The screen goes dark.

"Whoa," is all I can say. I slide the datastore out of the wall.

"So," Nola says, "I guess she's not the Mandate spy?"

"No," says a sharp voice behind us. "She's not a spy. She's being blackmailed."

"Sirra!" Nola nearly shrieks.

Sirra floats in the middle of the hall, her one leg still covered in marshmallow padding, though she's ditched the dressing gown for pants and shirt. Her face is almost as masklike as the man in the video.

"So that's what it was all about?" I ask. "The sneaking around and making secret off-ship communications in the middle of the night?"

Sirra stares at me. "I'd like my datastore back." She holds out her hand.

"And the midnight jump? Was that you, too?"

She gives a short nod. "There aren't a lot of places you can withdraw the amount of hard credit I needed without someone noticing. Hasoo-Pashtung is one of them."

I shake my head, trying to make sense of it. "But if you're not the Mandate spy, why did you care about getting me alone?"

Sirra snorts. "I wasn't trying to get *you* alone. As if you'd be any help. It was Nola I needed. I thought a Tech might be able to do something, and she's the best, so I was going to ask . . ."

"I could!" Nola pipes up. "I could track them down on the net, maybe even make a hunter app to go after the data itself. I'll start working on—"

"No!" Sirra shouts, her mask crumpling, making her look suddenly younger. She also looks angry, which doesn't surprise me, and terrified, which does. "I've had enough help from the two of you. I'm better off on my own. I'll pay what they want, and then this will all be over. And you are never, *ever* going to speak about it again. Especially not to Etander. Got it?"

"Got it," I say. "Here."

Sirra stares for a long moment at the nub of black

and gray in my outstretched palm. She raises a hand, but she doesn't take it. She makes a fist, and as her fingers clench, the datastore crumples, collapsing in on itself.

When it's the size of a gumball, Sirra drops her hand, turns around, and walks away.

CHAPTER 18

Captured

I SIT ON MY BED, staring at the metal gumball. A flock of images circles my thoughts. Sirra in the hallway, Rjool gloating over my secrets, Nyl with the Tinkers' Treasure in his hands. My own face in the mirror, pink-haired and hopeful, full of grand dreams of being a star. The Ringmaster telling me the truth.

If I sit very, very still, and try really hard, I can drive them away. The sound of Nola typing at her keypad grows dull, the world turns gray, but I'm still in control. I can't afford to break apart. I have a mission.

"Okay, that ought to do it," says Nola, catching another datastore as it ejects from the wall. "All we need to do is get this to an unprotected netlink and upload it. It'll search out any data matching the parameters I gave it and destroy them. Of course, the blackmailers might have an off-grid backup. But hopefully the hunter app can find them first and cause them enough trouble that they'll think twice about messing with Sirra."

"Sirra was right. You are the best," I say, still rolling the marble in my palm. "Feel any less guilty?"

Nola sighs. "Nope. You?"

I shake my head. "I've racked up enough bad karma at this point I'm coming back as a slug, even if we take care of Sirra's blackmailer. So where do we find an unprotected netlink?"

"That's the trouble. There aren't any, not in public. Only in Core Governance Communication offices, under high security."

"I guess that's my part, then. Is there one here?"

"On Hasoo-Pashtung? Yes, I think so. But we need a plan, Trix; you can't just walk in. And you saw the announcements this morning. We're leaving this sector after tonight's show."

I thunk my head back against the wall and groan. "Just once, I'd like something to work out. We've got no lead on Nyl and the rock, and no way to fix this mess with Sirra." *And you still don't belong here,* hisses a nasty voice in the back of my brain. *Maybe you ought to give up and go home.*

"There's one thing I don't understand," says Nola. "I can see Nyl managing to sneak into the Big Top during the show. It's not hard to lose one Mandate agent in a crowd of five thousand. But how did he know it was you, with the image projector on? If Sirra wasn't the spy, could it be someone else? Or *something* else?"

"You mean like a bug? Electronic surveillance?"

Nola bounces up and starts rooting around in her tool drawer. A few minutes later, the room is filled with the stench of hot metal and she's holding up a black wand trailing a spray of wires. She fiddles with a dial along one side of the thing. "There, this ought to detect any odd transmissions. We'll take it to the stage area and see if we find any—oh."

"What? Isn't it working?"

Nola looks up with big eyes. "Yes. And it's registering a signal. Here."

She starts waving the thing around the room, running it over the walls, the beds, even her *Love Among the Stars* poster. I hastily join her, peering over her shoulder at the bug sniffer. There's a small lighted display with a bar of light that wavers up and down as Nola directs the device around the room.

"Check our clothes. Maybe they planted something on us in the bazaar?" I pull out my jacket, still emblazoned with the silvery trophies from my high scores at the arcade. "Check the ribbons!"

She holds the wand to my jacket, but the display doesn't change. "It's not the ribbons." Nola shakes her head, setting purple sparks glittering.

I stare at her. "Here, let me try something."

Taking the bug sniffer, I raise it up to Nola's head. The red bar gets bigger and bigger, and the thing starts beeping like an insane microwave. I'm pointing it straight at the purple fiber-optic swatch she's been wearing ever since Jom said he liked it. The one I gave her. The one that guy at the bazaar gave me.

Nola tears it out of her hair and checks the readout. Then she stares at me. In a rush of motion she flings herself over to her drawer, pulls out an opaque black jar, thrusts the purple hair swatch into it, then slams the lid on it. "Give me an hour," she says. "I'm thinking our luck has changed."

A half-hour later, Nola is muttering under her breath and looking bloody murder at the fiber-optic bug. But she won't rest, and she won't give up. "If they're watching, they know we're onto them," she says. "We don't have long to track them down."

Another half-hour and Nola's got a dusting of metallic powder across her nose and singe marks up one arm, but she's grinning like a mad scientist. "That'll do the trick!"

I check out her newest creation, which looks a lot like a divining rod, except for the rippling lines of electricity that fill the V between the two metal arms. "What is it?"

"It should allow us to locate the receiver for that bug. There must be a relay somewhere nearby, probably out in the bazaar."

"Brilliant! Let's go!" I move for the door.

"Wait, Trix. Shouldn't we tell someone?"

I hesitate. The thought of facing the Ringmaster right now twists my stomach. Besides, it's not like we're after trouble. Just information. "No. We'll look like idiots if we bring a whole war party and there's nothing to find. Don't worry; it's a reconnaissance mission. No heroics, I promise. If we find them, we'll come back for help."

We head out into the bazaar, which is as crowded as ever. I plow into the throngs, giving Nola some space to do her thing. I try to hold my tongue, but after we pass by Supulu's for the third time, I have to ask, "Is it working?"

"Can't get a decent fix," Nola says, grimacing at the divining rod. "Time to try something else." She pulls a fist-size disk out of her pocket, twists a dial on the front, and hands it to me. "Take that. You'll have to get a good distance away from me, though."

"Why? What's it do?"

"It'll help triangulate the receiver location. I left one at the Big Top, too."

"Got it. I'll head for the spice market. Stay in touch."
I flick on my know-it-all.

"Be careful, Trix," she says. "Remember why we're here. Reconnaissance. Don't go picking fights."

"Who, me?" I wink as I head off down a side street, following the scent of alien spices.

I convince my know-it-all to show me our locations, overlaid on a map of the bazaar. The triangle between the Big Top, Nola, and me covers about a quarter of the region. "Needle in a haystack," says Britannica, "isn't that the saying on your planet? You really ought to go back and speak to the Ringmaster, dear."

I ignore her. "Hey, Nola, you see anything?"

Nola's voice crackles in my ear. It sounds like she's standing next to a racecar revving its engine. "Sorry for the—*rrrpphsst*—outdoor concert. It's crazy! But I think I've got—*vvrrrroooshhht*—getting a reading nearby!"

"Good work! I'm on my way. Hang back, though, Nola. Reconnaissance, remember?"

"*Wrrrrr*—here somewhere—*squeeee!*—very close!"

The sudden silence is almost a physical blow. "Nola? Nola?"

On the viewscreen, the light marking Nola's position suddenly winks out.

"Nola?" There are screams hidden in my voice, but I won't let them out. This isn't happening. "Britannica, where is she?"

"Dear me. Miss Ogala's know-it-all has gone offline."

I'm already sprinting, taking the fastest route I can find to the spot where she disappeared. Please be there, Nola. Please let it be the concert interfering with the signal. *Please.*

The square is jammed with people, rocking out to the racecar band. I search for Nola. Nothing. I keep moving, fighting my way to the light fountain at the center of the plaza. A lanky ebony-carved figure rises from the pool of luminescence, showers of color falling from its hands to dapple everyone and everything in rainbow light. I'm about to hoist myself up onto the statue's shoulders when I catch sight of something shiny on the flagstones. I jump down from the ledge of the pool to snatch it up.

It's the divining rod.

A roll of thunder drowns the caterwauls of the band. All around me people point, gesturing at the sky. I turn, following the fingers, to see a familiar sleek black ship rocketing into the heavens. Nyl's ship.

Nyl's got her. The Mandate has Nola.

* * *

"What's there to talk about?" I sputter. "We have to rescue her!"

"I simply said we would do well to consider the best course of action," says Miss Three coolly.

"I guess I shouldn't expect somebody with no heart, and no body for that matter, to get riled up. But I don't get why *you're* just standing there," I say, turning on the Ringmaster.

"I assure you I am doing considerably more than that." He speaks through gritted teeth. I recognize, belatedly, the look of intense concentration on his face as he stands with hands splayed across the console. We're on the bridge, which is where Britannica led me when I came rampaging back onto the ship less than ten minutes ago.

"Shouldn't we follow them?" I say, jittering my toes against the floor. "We need to do something."

"It seems to me you've done quite enough, Miss Ling," says Miss Three.

"Don't you think I know that?" My voice echoes from the walls, so hot it should be raising sparks. "I figured if they went for anyone, it'd be me. They *should* have come after me. I'm the expendable one."

Miss Three's thin lips twitch. "At least we agree on something."

"Enough." The Ringmaster's words crack like a whip. "We're about to jump. I suggest you prepare yourselves." The lights blink to orange as the compaction bell begins to toll a warning.

I hastily slide into one of the flip-out chairs, remembering with a twist in my gut that it was Nola who first showed them to me. "So we *are* going after them?"

"No. They're too far ahead, and the Big Top isn't prepared for an out-and-out fight in any case. We need more information. So we're going to visit informative friends."

"You mean to seek the Outcasts?" asks Miss Three. "Ringmaster, I must protest. They are too far outside our sphere. Their ways are too different. You cannot hope—"

"Yes, Miss Three, I can." The lights blink to purple. I stiffen, gripping my armrests as the sickening sensation of reality turning inside out takes over, and everything fades to black.

CHAPTER 19

The Outcasts

WE WAIT FOR THEM ONSTAGE. Even partially compacted, it's still the biggest space on the Big Top. The entire troupe is here to meet our mystery guests. We've been docked to their vessel for what feels like hours. I pace between the bleachers, keeping my distance from the others.

"It's only been thirty-point-four-five minutes," says my know-it-all. "Have some patience. Why don't you go sit with your friends?"

"Haven't you been paying attention? I lost my only friend. And anyway, I don't belong here."

Britannica tsks me. "My, my, it sounds to me like someone's feeling guilty. You belong here as much now as you ever did. Open your eyes, dear."

"Whatever. We're wasting time," I grumble, sticking my hands in my pockets and leaning against the railing. Something cool and metallic meets my hand, and for a moment I think it's the rock. I pull out the datastore with the hunter app, the one Nola made for Sirra before getting taken.

I look for Sirra, expecting to find her sitting pretty with her court of Principals in attendance. When I finally spot her, she's up on top of one of the bleachers, sitting with Etander and talking quietly and intently.

On the way up the stairs, I catch bits of their conversation.

"—should have told me," Etander is saying. He's not Hedgehog Boy, but he's on his way, flushed and tight-lipped.

"I'm taking care of it," Sirra retorts. "It's got nothing to do with you."

"It's my fault! We went to those doctors because I couldn't control—" He sees me and breaks off.

I clear my throat. "Hey. Sirra, can I talk to you?"

She's breathing fast, her fingers driving into the spongy stuff covering her leg, leaving deep dents. "I doubt it's anything I want to hear."

"Okay, don't listen. But take this." I hold out the datastore.

"What is it?" She narrows her eyes at me.

"Nola made it. To help with your . . . problem." I flick a look to Etander. "She said it needs to get uploaded on an unsecured netlink port. Dunno where you can find something like that, but I figure with your connections, you've got a better shot than me. Anyway, she wanted to help. So here. Take it."

I turn and retreat down the stairs as a distant clang shivers through the air. The whispers start the next moment. *They're here. The Outcasts.*

Returning to my skulking spot between the bleachers, I survey the crowd. Some look excited. Others look worried or afraid. Even the Ringmaster looks nervous. The door opens.

I take a step back. Talk about stage presence!

There's a vibe you get when someone is performing and you can feel that they're trying to reach out. You know they're performing to *you,* that everything is connected. It's why I still can't help but seek out the Ringmaster's gaze, even as angry and ashamed as I am right now.

The Outcasts aren't like that. They don't care what we think. At all. They want us to take a step back, to look away. They want us to *disconnect.*

There are three of them. The one in front is in his late teens maybe, with a topknot of white-blond hair that sweeps down over his black patch-elbowed duster. On his right hulks something I can't even identify, except that it's big and ugly. It moves with a wheezy groan of hydraulics, swiveling its metallic faceplate to take in the gathered crowd. A lump clogs my throat as I spot a patch of skin near the shoulder, oddly shiny and red. It's not a robot. It's a man, burned and buried under layers of metal.

The third Outcast is a girl. Her pigtailed hair bristles with metal skewers that I'm guessing are more than just decorative. And she's blue. All over. Trust me; her outfit doesn't leave much room for doubt on that point.

All three of them are painted and tattooed with sharp swirls of black and white and dripping with heavy metal chains and studs. It's a little over-the-top, but they pull it off without looking like rejects from a bad post-apocalyptic movie. Mostly.

The Ringmaster dips his top hat to the trio. "Welcome home, Reaper."

"This isn't my home," says the blond one, "not anymore. Looks like you've found plenty of new blood, though." He surveys the bleachers. Someone gives a half-wave. Reaper doesn't react. "I'm glad to see the old girl's still in one piece." He looks around the stage like a kid checking out his nursery, fond and disdainful.

"Barely," mutters Pigtails, around a gob of chewing gum. Tell me the blue girl did not just diss the Big Top in front of the Ringmaster.

"Ringmaster, this is Amp," says Reaper.

The blue girl gives the Ringmaster a look that makes me flush. "Mmm, the ship may be nothing to look at, but the captain's not bad. I could get used to sequins."

I'm indulging a colorful fantasy involving Amp and a few dozen space leeches when she snaps her gum. The crack is as loud as a bolt of thunder. I guess her superpower is more than blue skin and the ability to wear minimal clothing. She seizes the Ringmaster's hand in hers, sidling closer. "I make things loud."

"Charmed, I'm sure." The Ringmaster slips free from her grasp and gives Amp a carefully measured smile. I'm not-so-secretly pleased to see her pouting. Guess that bad-girl schtick isn't working the way she hoped.

Meanwhile, the Ringmaster has moved on to the third Outcast. Metal squeals against metal as the giant raises one bulky hand to flip up his faceplate.

I'm not the only one who hisses in surprise and—I'll admit it—disgust. The face beneath is a mass of scars and raw, flaking skin. The scarred man bows, stiff as a soldier. "Ringmaster, I have long aspired to the privilege of meeting you. We may have chosen differing paths, but there is none who can say you have not sacrificed all for our people. My name is Schadenfreude."

What the blazes? This translator must have a screw loose. I sure hope my name doesn't translate into something weird like that.

"That is a refreshing sentiment, Mr. Schadenfreude,"

says the Ringmaster. "And I'm grateful to all of you for agreeing to this meeting. I wouldn't have risked contacting you had the need not been very great."

"I haven't forgotten my debt," says Reaper. "But there's not much to go on in the details you sent. What makes you think we know where she is?" Reaper flicks a cool look at Miss Three, who's been hovering silently in the Ringmaster's shadow. "You've got an expert on the Mandate here. Good chance for her to finally earn her keep."

"I've already stated my opinion," says Miss Three. "The girl is beyond our reach. In all likelihood she's already dead, or converted."

"No!"

My shout is still echoing from the heights as I bound up into the Ring to confront them. "We're getting Nola back."

The Ringmaster, courteously smooth as usual, presents me with a wave of his baton. "Reaper, Miss Amp, Mr. Schadenfreude, this is our newest troupe member, Beatrix Ling, of Earth. She is also Miss Ogala's roommate and was in the vicinity when the abduction took place."

Amp snorts. "You couldn't stop them from taking her, and you think you're going to be able to get her back from inside a maximum-security Core station? Good luck with that."

"I'll get her back from a black hole if I have to," I snap, taking a step toward the blue girl. "Watch me."

Amp draws one of the steel needles from her hair. The Ringmaster tugs me back by one elbow. At a look from Reaper, Amp starts cleaning her nails with the thin spike.

"A Core Governance facility?" asks the Ringmaster. "But she was taken by an agent of the Mandate."

Reaper grimaces. "You see what happens when you spend your time pandering to a universe full of mindless drones? You're never going to do it, Ringmaster. They don't want to be saved. You've wasted too much effort on them already, when you could have been helping our own kind. If you had, maybe the girl would still be free."

The Ringmaster grips his baton, white-knuckled. "Let's put aside the philosophical debate for a time of greater leisure, shall we? Please, tell us what you know."

It's Schadenfreude who speaks then. "According to our sources, agents of the Mandate have infiltrated some of the highest levels of the Core Governance. They do not control it, though that may be their ultimate goal. But there are certain facilities under their total or near-total control."

"Circula Fardawn Station?" asks the Ringmaster.

"So you have been paying attention," says Reaper with a feral grin. "Yes, that was a blow the Mandate won't soon forget."

"Nor will the families of those who died there," says

the Ringmaster. "Or are you going to tell me all 567 sentients on that station were agents of the Mandate?"

"Collateral damage is part of war."

"That wasn't war. That was terrorism."

Reaper's lips curl. Amp starts tapping her skewer against one of her wide metal bracelets with a *ting, ting, TING* that's loud enough to rattle my bones.

"Enough," snaps Reaper. "I'm here to repay a debt. We have word that a prisoner was delivered to the station at Vargalo-5, and that the incoming flight originated from Hasoo-Pashtung. If that's not your girl, I don't know where she is. But Ringmaster, for once I agree with Miss Three. This isn't a fight you're going to win. Even the Outcasts aren't ready to take on Vargalo-5. It may look like a Core station and play by the Core rules, but it's Mandate through and through."

"We are fairly certain it's their main research facility," adds Schadenfreude. "We've . . . lost some of our own to that place."

My lips are stiff as cardboard, but I force the question out. "Lost, as in dead?"

"Not always. More often changed. Conformed. Broken." Schadenfreude shakes his head. His eyes are two pools of sorrow in a desert of twisted flesh and jagged metal.

"Then I guess we'd better get moving. Right?" I turn to the Ringmaster.

"Yes, of course. I've already plotted a route to the

Jorlax Nexus. If I can gain an audience with the right people, I'm sure we can arrange sufficient political pressure to—"

"*Political* pressure? They might be melting Nola's brain right now, and you want to chitchat? We need to go get her out!"

"I like this one," says Reaper. "Maybe she belongs with us."

"Yeah? And what are you going to do about Nola?" I ask.

His superior smile wavers. "We have plans to deal with Vargalo-5, eventually."

"Great. Another contender for the Who Can Be Most Useless title."

Reaper laughs. "You'd better watch her, Ringmaster. She'll give you almost as much trouble as I did."

"Oh, a good deal more, I suspect. She isn't a coward."

"Careful." Reaper's voice is low and dangerous. "I'm not your painted puppet anymore. I'm more powerful than you remember."

I stare at the Outcast. Was his long coat always that dark? Were there always drifts of shadow swirling around his feet? No, I'm not imagining it. They're moving, slithering along the floor toward the Ringmaster and me. With a suddenness that makes me gasp, my feet go numb. There are dim cries of alarm, but my world has turned dull and gray. I try to move, but everything is ice and stone.

"More powerful, yes," says the Ringmaster, "but no wiser."

Light bursts, brighter and brighter, burning into my eyes and bringing color to the world again. I blink, tears stinging from the brilliance, to see the Ringmaster brandishing his baton like a sword. Every light in the entire tent is blazing.

Reaper retreats, raising one hand to shield his eyes. When I blink again, there are no strange shadows darkening the floor. "We're done here," growls Reaper. Spinning on his heel, he heads for the door. Amp snaps her gum one more time, then follows.

The rest of the troupe are on their feet, chattering and calling out and stumbling woozily down from the bleachers. Whatever Reaper did, it affected everyone, though it looks like Theon made it halfway to center stage before getting knocked loopy. Jom's helping her up. I spot Gravalon Pree and Ghost, of all people, blocking the doors.

"Step aside, Gravalon, Ghost," calls the Ringmaster. "Let them go. The show's over."

Reaper and Amp leave and don't look back. Good riddance.

Schadenfreude still hasn't moved. "My apologies for the conduct of my associates," he says, dipping his head with a rasp of protesting metal. "I'm afraid you bring out the worst in him, Ringmaster. Even as you bring out the best in others." It takes me a minute to identify the grotesque spasm that crosses his face as a smile.

He turns to me. "I hope you can recover your friend unharmed. Perhaps this will help." He holds out a battered datastore. "This is all the information we've gathered on the station itself."

I take it, trying not to flinch as my fingers brush the cracked flesh and warped metal mosaic that is his palm. Schadenfreude flips down his faceplate, salutes the Ringmaster, then follows after the other Outcasts. The door closes behind them.

The Ringmaster sighs. "Relieved?" I ask.

"No. Regretful." He shakes himself. "But we've places to go and people to see. Move smartly, you lot. We'll be jumping to the Jorlax Nexus as soon as I'm back to the bridge."

What? Still?

Nods and calls of *Yeah!* and *Got it!* percolate through the rest of the troupe. "What about Vargalo-5?" I say loudly as the Ringmaster heads backstage.

He halts, shoulders slumping slightly. "Beatrix, I want to rescue Nola as much as you do, but there are better ways to go about this."

"I thought the whole point of this circus was to fight back. Isn't it?"

"Yes! I mean, no, not that way. It's more complicated than that. This isn't a battleship. It's a school, a home, a hope for the future."

"Then we leave the Big Top somewhere safe. We go there and get her out!"

"I . . . can't do that, Beatrix. My first duty is to keep this troupe safe."

"That worked real well for Nola." It's a cheap shot. I regret it as soon as the words are past my lips.

He whirls around with a terrifying suddenness. "I wasn't the one who led her into danger!" The fury in his voice tears into me.

I stagger back, gulping down air, digging fingernails into my palms. Stay focused. And damn it, do *not* cry. The acid of my guilt and anger churns through my veins, chewing at my insides. With visible effort, the Ringmaster relaxes, although the knuckles gripping his baton remain white and hard as diamonds.

"You're right," I croak, finding half my voice. I cough, but the lump in my throat won't go away. "I'm sorry. I know I messed up with the Firedance, but this isn't about showing off. This is about getting Nola back before they destroy her."

The Ringmaster lifts his head. There's something fragile in his eyes. When he speaks, his voice is a whisper. "I know. And if I could . . ."

I remember our trip to the Lighthouse, how he

checked that pocket watch, and the guilt on his face when he looked back at the Big Top. Then later, coughing like he was . . . like he was at death's door. He would get Nola back, if he could. But he *can't*. The realization staggers me.

"You can't leave the Big Top," I say, speaking low so only he can hear it. "When we went to the Lighthouse, it wasn't the atmosphere making you sick. It was being away from the Big Top. That's what you meant about choices and sacrifice. Being the Ringmaster means you can't leave her."

He lowers his gaze so I don't need to see what's breaking inside of him. "Not for long. Not for long enough to save Nola. I'm sorry."

I reach out and grip his hand, just for a moment. "That's all right," I say, loud enough so everyone can hear. "I'll save her. And I just might get the Tinkers' Treasure back, too."

My attempt at bravado misses the mark. He reaches for my arm. "Beatrix, no. That isn't what I meant. It's too dangerous. I can't let you to risk yourself that way."

"Don't worry." I'm all business now. Time to get this over with. "This is for the best. Your job is to keep the Tinker-touched safe. Not half-Mandate screwups who do more harm than good."

Startled exclamations batter my ears: Theon telling me not to joke, Jom insisting it's not true. Even Sirra looks surprised. Only Miss Three seems happy.

I take one long look around, fixing the stage in my memory, only the good parts. The sweetness of the cheers for my one-and-only performance. The Ringmaster blazing that heart-stopping smile, just for me, the first night I stepped onto this ship. Nola, being a better friend than I can ever deserve.

I have to remember it all. I don't expect to be back.

*   *   *

I spend the next twelve hours going through the information on the datastore from Schadenfreude. It's going to be tough; that's for sure. The Vargalo-5 station has security I've never even heard of. Gravimetric field inducers. Multiphase laser grids. Vuolu scent hounds. If I had a month to plan and a crack team of ninjas, I might stand a chance. Instead I've got a few hours, a soap-opera-addicted know-it-all, and me, the pink-haired wonder.

I've got to give Britannica credit, though. I don't know if it's all the *Love Among the Stars* or what, but she's got one devious mind hidden in those microchips. Between the two of us, we cook up a pretty decent plan. There's only one problem with it.

"Aaaaugh!" I throw my viewer onto the bed. "There must be some way onto the station. Maybe I can get close enough to use spacewings. Or find a transport to sneak onto. You guys have pizza delivery, don't you?"

"Let's stay focused on rational options, dear. Now,

have you considered disguising yourself as a snappy, up-and-coming junior officer of the Core Governance? Dalana does that in season twelve, episode thirty-two, in order to liberate the scientist wrongly convicted of espionage."

"I'm so glad we're sticking to rational options." I groan and flop onto the bed. Maybe I ought to sleep. But we'll be docking at the Jorlax Nexus in less than an hour. That's my one shot. I've got to have a plan ready for action. Maybe I should ask the Ringmaster for help. Then again, he might just try to stop me. We haven't spoken since the Outcasts left. I wish—

The door chime pulls me back from these thoughts. Finally! I spring up, race to the door, and slap my palm on the pad. My pulse thrums loud in my ears. "Ringmaster, I—Jom? What are you doing here?"

I search the hall, but there's no one else. Jom runs a hand back over his crest of red hair, looking sheepish. "I'm here to help. You're going after Nola, right?"

"Um, yeah, but—"

"Then I'm going with you." He pulls his shoulders back. A whiff of some sharp, minty scent hits my nose. "I'm not letting them change her. I don't care how dangerous it is."

"Are you sure? That was the truth, what I said in the Ring. About who I am."

"You're her friend. You're not abandoning her. That's

what really matters. Besides, the way the Ringmaster explained it to us, you're a Tinker, too. The Big Top let you in, and that's good enough for me. And . . ." He crinkles a smile at me. "I've got the perfect way to get onto Vargalo-5. So what do you say?"

"Ask him if it involves disguises," pipes Britannica. I ignore her and stick out my hand.

"I say welcome to the Nola Liberation Army. So, tell me about your plan . . ."

CHAPTER 20

EScape

BY THE TIME we do dock at the Jorlax Nexus, I'm feeling almost chipper. Jom's plan is . . . innovative . . . but it's better than nothing. I'd feel better with a few ninjas, but I'll take what we've got.

The Ringmaster never does come calling, at least not in person. Britannica takes a couple of short voice messages, and then one long one. They're all variations on a theme: Please stay here. Stay safe. Diplomatic channels. Time. I delete them before they make me chicken out.

A half-hour after we dock, the Ringmaster is deep

into negotiations with his contacts, and it's time for Jom and me to make our move. We head for the airlock that links ship to station.

"Looks clear," I say.

We make it about three steps when a ghostly figure shimmers into focus, barring the way.

"Miss Ling, I've been expecting you," says Miss Three. "The Ringmaster suspected you would not listen."

"Trix," says Jom in a low voice, "we need to get to the distribution center by twenty-one hundred hours or this won't work."

"Get out of our way, Three." I step forward. "Or I swear I'll find your motherboard and stomp it into itty-bitty pieces."

She arches a perfect brow at me, then glides to one side. "You mistake me. I'm not here to stop you. Go. This ship is better off without you. *He* is better of without you." Then she's gone, winked out.

"Let's go!" Jom pulls me out the door.

After the Hasoo-Pashtung Bazaar, the Jorlax Nexus station is a little disappointing. It reminds me of an airport, or one of those old indoor shopping malls, with stands selling JoJoPop and Supulu's Scoops every fifty feet and bubbly, inoffensive music piped in. The people look like regular sorts, out for a stroll, on business, shopping. The view, though—that's pretty freaking amazing. If I survive the next six hours, I am definitely coming back here. The outer walls are clear, floor to ceiling. On the other side is a Hubble image come to life. Not as colorful, maybe, but much, *much* bigger. Swirls of bronze and gold filter the light of a dying star. It's a sight to hold on to.

We hit our first roadblock, literally, when we're about halfway to our destination. A security checkpoint chokes the flow of traffic to a standstill. There's a single archway that I take to be a high-tech metal detector, and the line waiting to pass through it must be a hundred people deep.

"Gotta love the Core Governance in action," says Jom, grimacing. "We've got ten minutes."

"You think we should jump it?"

"I'm sure you'd love another chance to show off," says a voice beside me. "But if you're serious about saving Nola, you're probably better off without the attention."

"Sirra?" Jom asks. "What are you doing here? Taking tea with the Wazeer of Deneb?"

He's right. She looks ready for a state event. The marshmallow cast has been replaced by a close-fitting brace that blends into her dark velvety pants. Her tall boots shine as if daring one speck of dust to land on them. Golden insignias glitter with gems, decorating her fitted scarlet coat. She's even wearing something that, I kid you not, looks like a tiara.

"You two clearly need help," she says. "And I need

an unprotected netlink upload site." She holds up Nola's datastore.

"So you want to come with us?" I say. "Risk everything?"

"I've got everything to lose if I don't do something," she says, clenching the datastore in her fist. "So, do you want to stand here all day or what?"

"I'll take the 'what' option," says Jom.

"Follow me, then, and keep your mouths shut." Sirra marches forward, limping slightly. Jom and I look at each other and abandon our spot in line.

Sirra's not even halfway to the checkpoint when the flurry of activity starts. The guards look as if someone set loose a swarm of bees on them, rushing back and forth, waving hands in the air. I spot one guy ducking behind a potted plant to tuck in his shirt and straighten his jacket. The excitement spreads to the people waiting in line, who point and watch open-mouthed.

By the time we reach the checkpoint, there's a line of uniformed guards standing at attention. They even *salute*. I'm starting to see how Sirra turned out the way she did, if this is the kind of treatment she's used to.

"Lady Centaurus," says a guard with a silver star on her cap, saluting again. "This is a great honor. We had no word that one of your family would be visiting the Nexus. Is the President traveling with you?"

"No, my mother isn't here. But I'm sure she would

be glad to know the security of Nexus is in such capable hands."

The guard looks so happy at this you'd think Sirra had handed her the winning lottery ticket and a puppy. Sirra continues on, "But I do have some *rather urgent* family business to attend to, if you understand."

"Oh, yes, of course, Lady Centaurus. You, there, clear a path. Quickly, now, let's not keep the lady waiting."

Sirra slips a coy look back at Jom and me, then resumes her regal coolness. Within a minute we're being waved past the checkpoint. Jom and I get some odd looks, mostly focused on our . . . unusual . . . hair. But one sweet little smile from Sirra and an "Oh, these are my assistants," and we're free and clear.

Sirra keeps up the empress-of-the-universe act until we round the next bend in the main walkway. Then she ducks into an alcove beside a potted palm. She pulls off the dozens of gold emblems and tiara and stuffs them into a pouch, then shakes the elaborate hairstyle down and ties it back in a simple ponytail.

"Please tell me you have a plan to get to Vargalo-5," Sirra says, fiddling with a tiny dial on the sleeve of her coat. As she spins it, the color of the jacket darkens from the brilliant scarlet to a muted burgundy. The empress is gone, replaced by a polished but not particularly eye-catching young woman.

"Can't you snap your fingers and get your minions to help?" I say as we head off down the walkway.

"Even I can't just walk into a high-security military research facility."

"Don't worry," says Jom, careening around a corner and leading us down a side hall. "I've got us our ticket to Vargalo-5 right here." He points ahead to the doorway emblazoned with the image of a gigantic ice cream cone and the words SUPULU'S SCOOPS DISTRIBUTION CENTER. Jom presses one hand across the identification panel. The door slides open with a cheery "Welcome, Master Supulu!"

We follow Jom into the chilly maze of shelves packed with tubs labeled Tachyon Toffee Swirl and Cosmic Crunch to a loading bay. A stubby shuttlecraft emblazoned with the Supulu logo and the words DELIVERY SERVICE sits proudly on the flight deck, being prepped by a crew of robotic loaders. As we watch, one of the mechanicals deposits a final pallet stacked with tubs into the delivery shuttle. Everything, from the tubs to the robots to the shuttle, is striped in pale green and lavender.

Jom comes out from the cockpit with a bundle of lavender and green fabric in his hands. "Um · I hope you guys like stripes."

* * *

I squirm in my seat, looking ne window at the
Vargalo-5 station below. The domes bubble up
from the blasted lunarscap small moon.

"Don't worry," says Jom from his spot at the controls. "There's another two transports ahead of us. We'll get our clearance eventually."

I blow out my breath, but it doesn't help with the tight feeling in my chest. The air in here is too thin. And this uniform isn't helping. "How do they expect you to work with this—this *thing* flopping into your face every time you turn around?" I try for the umpteenth time to reposition the peaked lavender and green cap so the pompom on the end isn't tickling my nose.

"Oh, it's not that bad," says Jom, giving the fluffy tip of his own hat a practiced flick to send it back over one shoulder. "My grandfather designed the uniforms, you know. The cap's supposed to look like an ice cream cone. Get it?"

"Enough of this," I mutter. Pulling off my cap, I give the pompom a good yank. It pops free. I toss it into the aisle.

In the seat across from me, Sirra's been waging her own war against the hat. She stops to watch the depomming. Catching my eye, she grins. A moment later her own cap is pompom free.

"And listen," says Jom, "I know this is a deadly dangerous mission and all that, but my uncle's going to kill me if anything happens to this stuff. So try to keep the uniforms clean you can. What? Why are you both giggling?"

Sirra slaps a hand over her mouth, but her shoulders keep shaking. I sweep the two discarded pompoms off the floor and make a show of dusting them off, which only makes Sirra laugh harder.

It's a weird, weird world. A week ago Sirra and I hated each other, and honestly, we probably still do. But right now I'm just glad to have someone to laugh with, to loosen the bands of fear that clamp me down whenever I think about what's coming.

Jom leans forward, taking the manual controls as a voice crackles from the comlink. "Supulu Shuttle 8552, please hold your position. We have an incoming flight that has priority."

I sink lower into my seat. Wonderful. More waiting.

"Copy that, Vargalo-5," replies Jom cheerfully. Then he lets a note of doubt into his voice. "I sure hope I don't lose any cargo, though. Freezers won't last much longer."

There's a pause. Then the same voice, but less clipped and formal. "You got any of that Limited Edition Love Among the Starberries on board?"

"Sure do!" says Jom. "Tell you what, if you can get us down sooner rather than later, I'll even set aside a pint for you."

There's another, longer pause, then "Supulu Shuttle 8552, you are cleared for descent to platform North Gamma-5. Please report to the deck officer upon landing."

"Thank you, Vargalo-5 Control," says Jom. He clicks off the comlink and winks back at Sirra and me. "Ice cream: better than a universal lockpick."

Jom works more of his magic on the deck officer after we land, distracting him with a tub that's "exceeded optimal storage temperatures" and can't be refrozen without violating some Supulu taboo. While the officer takes an ice cream break, we get to supervise the unpacking of the remaining tubs.

The moment the guard is out of sight, I head for the nearest com station. Sirra beats me to it, only to slam a fist into the wall. "Internal only! No netlink. It's not enough."

"It's enough for me." I edge around her and flick on my know-it-all. "Britannica? You in?"

"Of course. Bringing up schematics now."

The screen blinks on, showing the now-way-too-familiar layout of the station.

"There," says my know-it-all over the shared com channel. "Miss Ogala is in the detention wing, as expected. Records indicate she has been subjected to only minimal processing."

"Thank the First Tinker," says Jom, jogging over to join us, having finished with the unloading.

Britannica goes on, "You should be able to proceed with the original plan of making your way around the outer maintenance passages and then . . . Oh, dear."

"What's wrong?"

"No . . . I mean, I don't know. It's too much. Changing too fast."

On cue, I slam back down to the floor. Jom bellows in pain.

"If I get it wrong, it might backlash. It could tear us all into pieces."

"If it's a choice between that and getting beaten to a bloody pulp, I'll take the chance," calls Jom.

"I don't think I can do it.".

"Come on, Sirra, you're the star of the Circus Galacticus. You perform for bazillions of people. You're the definition of overachiever. Everything you do is perfect. Believe me; I noticed. So do this! Get another ⏤ star for your collection."

Nothing. I think I hear her breathi⏤ desperate.

"I'm afraid Lady Centaurus ⏤ further assistance," pipes my k⏤ you can reach that contro⏤ chamber?"

I'd laugh, but there's no air ⏤ move an inch, let alone cross the ⏤ But I try. Not much else to do. "I gu⏤ one thing I can do better, though," I say. ⏤ giving up without a fight."

Sirra's voice is faint. "You're trying to ⏤ angry."

"Well, yeah," I admit.

"I'm afraid Miss Ogala is scheduled to be transferred to a treatment chamber in approximately thirty-three minutes."

"What kind of treatment?" asks Sirra.

"Full-scale genetic cleansing."

"Even in a best-case scenario, our planned route will take forty," says Jom. He pulls off his cap and twists it so roughly I hear a rip. "And the backup plan isn't much better."

"Then we'd better find a backup for the backup." I glare into the sea of thin green lines that stand between me and Nola. I point to the schematics. "Look here, there's a passage that runs almost straight from where we are to the detention block. It's the only way."

"That's the passage with the Vuolu scent hounds," says Jom, continuing to mangle his hat.

"You said you had a way to get past them."

"I said I had an idea. That's not the same thing. And I can't do anything about the variable gravimetric fields."

"Good thing we've got Gravity Girl with us, then."

I point to a spot near the blinking light that marks Nola's cell. "And look, Sirra, you're in luck: There's a full netlink station right here."

Sirra doesn't move. For a moment I ⏤nk I might have to come up with an inspiring sp⏤h. Then she shakes herself, gives a tight nod, and ⏤ds for the w⏤ panel that leads to our backup back⏤ route.

The first part is tense and b⏤s, not a good ⏤

67
☆

binación. All we find are seemingly endless tubelike passages that make me feel like a gerbil. We scuttle along
the Habitrail, hunched and ready for attack, for sirens
and wailing alarms. It's a dangerous feeling when you
start hoping for something to happen to relieve the
numb fear slowly paralyzing your thoughts.

I notice the tube widening, feel an odd heaviness
in one foot. Britannica starts to say something, but it's
too late. Suddenly my entire body has turned to lead.
I slam down onto the floor. A hum of power buzzes in
my bones.

"Graphimephric . . . m-field," says Jom, the translator barely un-garbling the words. With great effort I
twist my head a fraction of an inch so I can see him
splattered flat as a pancake against the floor.

"Sirra," I gasp out. "Your . . . cue."

The field shifts sickeningly. Is this how the ocean
feels in a storm? Whipped by waves that shift it and sh
it around until up is down and inside is out? I
teeth, my entire focus boiling down to o

Don't hurl.

When it stops, I'm on the cei
have bec.me clouds. Jom car

"Sirra! Do.mething!"

I twist ...he mo
.e around to
.r dark ha
fri.

"It's working." The words are sharper, stronger.

I can't see what's happening, but suddenly my body
feels cloudlike again. Jom groans. "Hold on," says Sirra.
"Don't move."

The clouds turn to marshmallows, then to solid flesh.
My heels sink onto the floor. I catch myself against the
wall. Don't hurl, don't hurl, chants my brain. Sirra flies
past and taps something into the control panel. The
humming stops.

"Good work," I say, once I find my lips. "Remind
me to give you that gold star."

Sirra smiles. "If we get out of here, it's gold stars all
around."

"Ah, isn't it wonderful how a little adversity can
make bosom friends out of former enemies?" says my
know-it-all in a dreamy voice.

I snort. "Bosom friends?"

"Hardly," says Sirra, dropping her smile like a hot
coal. "Let's call it allies for now."

"Sounds good to me." I move to join Jom over at
the hatch that will take us out into the detention wing.

"I'll go first," he says. "If there are Vuolu hounds,
I'll distract them. You two get Nola out. Okay?"

"As long as distracting them doesn't mean letting
them chew on you."

"No." Jom cracks the hatch, peering out. "But it
does involve a bit of acrobatics and making myself smell

like a fresh Denebian sausage. Nothing a Clown can't handle. All right, it's clear." He ducks out of the hatch.

Sirra and I follow, emerging into a gray corridor lined with narrow doors that remind me uncomfortably of tombstones. It takes me a moment to get oriented. "It should be this way," I say, pointing to the right.

"Shhh!" Jom raises a warning hand. In the silence that follows, the *click-click-click* of claws echoes from somewhere around the corner to the left. "Go! Find her!"

Then he's gone, slipping off down the left-hand hall, trailing a faint whiff of smoked meat. I hesitate. It feels wrong, but we're running out of time.

"You heard him," Sirra says.

We move on. I'm listening so hard for growling and screaming in the distance, I miss the cell. Sirra catches my elbow and points to the number glowing from the keypad beside the nearest door. "This is it."

"And there's the netlink." I point up the hall. "Go do your thing." Leaning closer to the door, I call out, "Nola?"

A long moment ticks by, and I swear I lose about a year of my life before I catch the faint "Trix? Is that really you?"

"Pink hair and all. I've got Jom and Sirra here, too. Don't ask; I can't explain it, either. We're here to rescue you, but we're going to need help. Can you get this door open? You know, with your Tech mojo?"

"I can try. But everything keeps spinning. Whooa, one step in front of the other." There's a muffled thump from inside the cell. "Hello, there, Mr. Door. How do you feel about opening? Good? Oh, do you really have to? Well, okay, then . . ."

The next moment the door slides open, Nola falls out, and sirens start blaring.

Sirra rejoins me, her face sharp with fear. "They're coming!" The thud of running footsteps pounds toward us.

Jom rounds the corner, running like he's got a pack of Vuolu hounds on his trail. Relief breaks over his face like a sunrise when he sees us. "You found her! Is she okay?"

"She's fine. Pretty loopy, though. I think they drugged her. She's not going to make it out on her own."

Jom doesn't hesitate. He scoops Nola up and keeps running. Sirra and I follow. We hurtle around the corner and skid to a stop. Three gray-uniformed soldiers block the hall, brandishing familiar stubby black weapons. Sirra sweeps her arms up, and suddenly all three are floating into the air. We duck under their flailing legs and race onward and into our hatch.

Gravimetric chamber, Habitrail, it all whips past now as we flee, driven by the shrieks of the alarms. I roll out the last panel into the landing bay and spring upright, fists clenched, ready to fight. But all I see is the striped

"No weapons," says the Ringmaster, his voice grim.

"No shields, either," adds Nola.

Syzygy stares at me. "Not yet."

I look down at my hand. Does she mean I should use the Treasure? Even Nyl said it. *All the power of the Tinkers' Touch, in your hand for the taking. It's what you wanted all along, isn't it? To be a brighter star than any of them.*

The first bolts are almost graceful, bursting from the wings of one of the enemy craft, arcing like a golden rainbow across the screen. Then the world spins, metal groans, and the entire Big Top shudders like an old woman caught in a cold, cold wind.

"Close call," Nola says, then cries a warning as three more missiles spin toward us.

"Hold on! It's going to—"

The impact throws me to the ground. The Ringmaster is the only one who keeps his feet. I doubt there's any power in the universe that could pull him from that console. I look at his face and wish I hadn't. He knows the Big Top is dying. And I know, with a certainty that shakes me to the core, that he's dying, too. She's a part of him, or he's a part of her. The details don't matter. He can't leave her. He can't live without her.

Warmth tugs at my hand. I look at the rock. The glossy blackness is cracked with lines of red and gold. Inside, a light pulses, beating like a trapped hummingbird.

A faint chiming calls to me. It wants to be used. It wants to grow into something new and glorious. It's there for me to take, if I want it, like Nyl said. The vision catches me with a suddenness that makes me gasp. I see myself, powerful, brilliant. Shining brighter than any star. I am the pinnacle of the Tinkers' art. The Tinkers' Treasure can save me.

But I'm not the one who needs saving. I close my smarting eyes. I don't know what to do. It's a gorgeous, dazzling dream but somehow . . . false. Because it's not only me. It's Nola, working her magic behind the scenes, showing up to help me even when I didn't deserve it. It's Sirra, sharp and hard as diamond, willing to risk everything for her brother. It's Jom and Theon and all of them, the madcap, rampaging, brilliant troupe. And it's the Ringmaster and his Big Top, coming to take me away, giving me a dream to believe in. A dream I *still* believe in.

Syzygy's voice breaks my reverie. "One thousand three hundred forty-nine. There is still time."

1349. The room the rock was leading me to. "I know what to do," I say, quietly at first, to myself more than anyone else. Then louder. "Ringmaster! I need to get to the Restricted Area. I know how to save the Big Top."

He doesn't ask questions, though I see them in his eyes. He takes my hand, turns, and runs for the door.

Five times we're thrown by the sudden tilting of the floor. I start to smell smoke. The Big Top shudders and

CHAPTER 22

Principles

I T'S STILL THE SAME old Big Top, even with a Tinkers' Treasure makeover. Sure, the doors are less wheezy, the lights shine a bit brighter, and the Techs say it'll take days to catalogue all the new defensive systems. But I still trip over piles of feather boas in the halls, and Nola's still the only one who can program the autosalon.

When I go to dinner the first night after it all went down, I prepare myself to sit alone. I figure it's better that way. Less attachments, less hurt when I go. I don't count on Nola, Jom, Theon, Gravalon, and a half-dozen others crowding around table five to join me. Jom even gives me the second-largest Chocolate Supernova for dessert, nearly as big as Nola's.

I won't lie. I love it. And hate it. They don't even say the word *Mandate,* but it's there, hanging in the air like the stench of a forgotten lunch, left to rot under the table. I let Jom tell the story of Nola's breakout, and when they ask what happened to me afterward, I shrug and mumble something about being questioned.

As if it were that easy.

* * *

There's one conversation I can't run away from, though, even if it scares me stiff. When I find the Ringmaster, he's looking out from the viewing deck at the whorls of light and color drifting past. In a strange way it makes me feel better. Last time we were standing here, my world was breaking apart and I was furious with him. Now it's time to put it back together and apologize.

"Hey," I say. "I've got something for you."

He turns, his expression scrupulously mild, like I'm a rabbit he expects to bolt. I hold out the pink teapot. "I'm sorry it's chipped," I say. "It kinda took a detour."

Yes, I went back and got it. From Rjool. And trust me, there's no power in the universe that's going to make me tell anyone that story. *Ever.*

groans. I run faster. By the time we get to the section with the corrugated walls, I'm leading the way. It's like the rock itself is a magnet, pulling me along, unerringly, to its destiny. Outside door 1349 I pause for a breath, then press my palm against the spongy surface. The door folds back in pleats. The room on the other side is nothing I could have imagined.

It's a little like stepping into a giant brain, complete with the ick factor. Except it's more than that. The curving walls shimmer with golden light. Ghostly images flicker at the corners of my eyes. Sparks glitter, leaping between the stalactite-like growths that decorate the room, if *room* is even the right word.

The Ringmaster stands motionless. "Beatrix," he says, "this is the heart—the brain—the soul of the Big Top. I always knew you had a heart of gold, old girl," he adds quietly.

A shudder shakes the room. The Ringmaster stumbles, nearly falling. He steadies himself against a stalagmite.

"Ringmaster?" Nola's voice comes over the com, cracking with fear. "They're all over the place! They keep coming and coming. I don't know what to do!"

"Nola," I say calmly, "it's going to be okay. Listen. You got that? Breathe." I look down one last time at the Tinkers' Treasure, pulsing in my hand like liquid gold. Then I throw it into the air.

It hangs for a moment, growing brighter and brighter.

With a tinkling like a roomful of breaking china, it explodes, scattering flakes of golden light. I rub my eyes, and when I look again the entire room is glowing, rippling. Changing. The walls tremble. My skin prickles, goose bumps rising. Even my scalp tingles.

The Ringmaster stands frozen, staring around in bewilderment as if someone just threw him a surprise party and it wasn't even his birthday.

"Where did that come from?" Nola's voice rises, alarmed. "The Big Top doesn't have shields. Or polarity-reversal canons. What's going o—ooooh! The Big Top has shields! Hah! And polarity-reversal canons! Yeah, you better run away, Mandate scum. And don't come back."

The Ringmaster looks between the teapot and me. Before he can say anything, I blurt it all out. "I'm sorry, Ringmaster. You took me up here, gave me all of this" —I wave out the window—"and I . . . I've been nothing but trouble. I'm so sorry." I study the pattern of the floor panels with such intensity that his touch on my arm makes me jump.

"Beatrix, the Mandate are the ones who want only to avoid trouble. Nyl and his ilk would have us all following rules blindly, accepting what we're given. I meant what I said to Reaper. I like a bit of trouble in my life." This time he doesn't wink when he says it. At that moment my elbow is my connection to everything that matters.

"If you hadn't acted when you did, Nola might have been lost to us, utterly. I hesitated. I was confused. I wanted to be sure. I was . . . afraid." His face darkens.

"You had more to lose. I get that now," I say, wanting to chase the shadows from his eyes. "It was easier for me to take the risk. I'm nothing sp—"

The word dies unspoken as the Ringmaster presses one finger to my lips. "No. I knew exactly what I was doing when I asked you to join the Circus Galacticus. Special isn't only what you can do. It's the choices you make. You don't go through the universe looking for a place that's ready-made for you to fit into, a round peg for a round hole. You have to make your own place. Do you understand?"

I nod, and his finger falls away, leaving a ghost of warmth. He sighs. "My mistake was not realizing I needed to do the same . . ."

"What do you mean?"

"I don't know what this is all for." The Ringmaster waves to the room. "The Tinkers left this ship for us, but for what purpose? Am I truly doing their work, gallivanting around the universe?"

All this time I've been thinking about how much I need this place, this life. I looked to the Ringmaster to show me the way. Now, suddenly, the world has shifted. There's a desperation in his eyes that kills me. "That's not the right question," I say. "Those ancient long-lost Tinkers, they're gone. They retired, quit, whatever. You're the one who's here now, reminding people they can reach the stars and choose their own destinies. That's the real way to fight the Mandate. That's the real way to bust those cages. And I think the universe needs that pretty badly right now. I—" My voice breaks. "I know I did."

He meets my gaze for a long moment, then nods as the terrible tension in his face ebbs away.

"So that's our place," I say, smiling. "That's what we do."

The Ringmaster's eyebrows rise toward the brim of his top hat. "We?"

"If you'll still have me. Even if I'm never more than a pink-haired-clown dancing-fruit person. This is where I belong."

"I'm . . . glad to hear it." There's a catch in his voice. The Ringmaster doesn't look at me, but I can almost feel the shape of the space between us, no longer filled with fear, but with possibilities.

He clears his throat and continues on breezily. "But don't abandon all hope. You had the Tinkers' Treasure in your hands. You may not have used its power for yourself, but that doesn't mean it hasn't left its mark. And then there's this."

He holds out a familiar, gold-filigreed book. The cover reads *The Programme of the Circus Galacticus, Thirteenth Edition*.

"Thirteenth? How? What changed?"

He grins, flipping it open. And there it is, at the bottom of the cast list.

"The Champion: She who guards the Dreamers and stands undaunted before the King of Iron and Flame." I skim the rest, not quite taking it in.

"No way. Really?"

"Unless you know someone else with a 'brave spirit and hair like a sunset sky,' I think there's little doubt who it's referring to. So," he adds, "Clown or Principal? You'd be within rights to trade in for a star." The Ringmaster's smile is a riddle, but I know the answer.

We stand there, our faces turned to the galaxies wheeling past. It's not the desert, and I can't forget what I've lost. But that's okay.

"I've got all the stars I need right here."

Acknowledgments

I wrote this book in an attempt to capture some of the wonder and awe I feel every time I look up at the stars. I would like to express my deepest thanks to the scientists, astronauts, and all the other men and women who have worked over the years to understand and explore our universe. I'd particularly like to thank (and recommend!) the folks behind www.astronomycast.com, who provide a wealth of fascinating, inspiring, and accessible information about all sorts of topics related to astronomy.

Many thanks are also due to Karen Jordan Allen, R. J. Anderson, Geoff Bottone, Melissa Caruso, Megan Crewe, Erin Dionne, Robert Dunham, Megan Frazer, Robin Merrow MacCready, Patty Murray, Cindy Pon, Jon Skovron, and Luanne Wrenn for reading various versions of this manuscript and helping me to make it better.

I remain grateful to my agent Shawna McCarthy for being my advocate and adviser, and to my editor Reka Simonsen for her wise insights and attention to detail. Many thanks to everyone who helped produce this book, including Sarah Dotts Barley, Ana Deboo, Su Box, and the team at Harcourt.

And last but not least, I thank my wonderful, amazing family. Mom, Dad, Dave, and my beloved Bob, thank you for your support. You are my stars!